Dodging Bullets
(Fiction based on actual events)

By

Kentrell Myers
& Michael Gerald

Blackkkash
1205 Charbonnet Street
New Orleans, LA 70117

Ordering Information:
For details, contact
kash9ward@gmail.com.

Print ISBN: 9781005700768
eBook ISBN: 9781005700768

Printed in the United States of
America on SFI Certified paper.

Intro

We live in a world that makes
perception reality. We make
decisions everyday based on
assumption. You can now tell the
truth, and people still won't
believe you. So what is the point of
lying?

For those who do not live in the
ghetto... like the politician's
making decisions about the ghetto,
the people you work with who do not
realize that you caught three buses
and a train, just to get to work
from the ghetto, or the people that
do limited research, but have all of
the answers about the ghetto, right
there in black and white. They can
only assume that they know what is
going on in the ghetto. A place
where a person can lose their life
just from their reputation.

Sometimes, an opportunity presents
itself to someone else, when another
person is killed in the ghetto. Just
like in the regular world, or
politics. If one can get away with a
murder, sometimes, that is the
reason a person is killed. Sometimes
it is mistaken identity. There are
plenty of answers to why people lose
their lives in the ghetto. Sometimes
you do get away with murder... at

least, until your luck runs out.
Some people are just lucky. But they
think they have the game all figured
out.

One may think that they know how to
move in the streets, especially when
they are so deeply embedded in the
streets. But at that point, the
streets have already chewed you up
and spit you out. Once you start
making money, you are now a target
for another person to come up off of
your death. You can do everything
right, and still lose your life.

When you are living in the streets,
at a certain point, you are no
longer the baby with the cute little
pinchable cheeks, or that kid your
mother raised.

This story takes place in the mean
streets of New Orleans, where they
hustle and do things a little
differently in the streets. Can you
imagine living life making money in
the ghetto? It is not like what you
see on T.V. Television is fake.

Let's take a deep dive into the
ghetto, where everyone thinks...
they have the game figured out, but
they are all just doing what they
have to do to survive. When their

reality, is not what it appears to
be.

Chapter 1

It is 3 am, and three teenage boys of color are leaving a house party drunk as hell. The nineteen-year-old driver, Corey, is just a little less tipsy than the other two, Troy, sitting in the front passenger seat, and Zap, in the back seat behind Corey.

Five minutes into the ride Corey notices an unknown car following them.

He alerts Troy and Zap. They begin to panic. Corey says, "Who the hell is following us?" Troy says, "Pullover". "Nigga is you crazy? Fuck no, you better not pull this car over," Zap replies.
"Why are they following us so close?" Corey continues.

Corey is now obsessively checking the rear and side-view mirrors as the car following them begins to flash its headlights and blow its horn. "Something is not right," he says.

"And his crazy ass wants us to pull over and see what they want," Zap utters, as he looks at Troy. Corey takes a peek into the rear-view mirror, and says, "Look they are turning off." "Who the fuck was that?" Troy asks. Zap sarcastically blurts out, "You want to go back and find out?"

Corey wastes no time getting them out of the area, and fortunately, everything goes well the rest of the way as the three teens make it home safe and sound.

The next morning, Lou, a man of color in his early to mid thirties, and his fiancé Trina, a woman of color that is a few years younger, or putting the finishing touches on hot passionate sex session, when Lou's cell phone rings.

It is Jason, one of his good friends. Lou answers the phone cheerfully, "What is up Homie?" "You were acting funny last night huh? Old scary ass Lou," Jason says.

Lou pauses with a confused look on his face before saying. "Jason, man, what the hell are you talking about?"

From the bathroom, Lou's fiancé, Trina, yells out loudly, "I need to go to the store to get some things for the house, and the party for Corey." Lou ignores her while he is on the phone. Then she says, "Lou I know you heard me."

Lou screams an irritated, "Ok!…", back to Trina. Lou, now speaking to Jason, "…my bad dog. She always doing that when I get on the phone it is like she waits for my phone to ring to ask me to do some shit." Jason, laughs aloud and says, "Boy I tell you, women… you can`t live with them, and you can`t hide shit from 'em." "Ain't that the truth," Lou continues while also laughing.

Jason says to Lou in a more serious tone, "Hey man let me call you back, my phone is ringing. I have been waiting on this call." Lou says, "Ok then, get back at me dude."

Lou hangs up the phone with Jason. Meanwhile, in the room down the hall from Trina and Lou`s bedroom, we find Corey, the teen driving the car last night, and Trina's lazy kid brother. He is blissfully knocked out sleeping.

Trina bursts into the room and yells "Get your ass up now! You will not sleep all day! You don't pay no damn bills." He does not move. "Get up Corey, I am not playing with you boy!" Corey is still trying to recover from last night.

Lou is in his bedroom laughing his ass off at Trina trying to awaken Corey, because he knows Trina is being messy.

Having a loved one pushing him to be great, or just to do better, is hard enough. Corey finally gets up, now Trina wants him to go and look for a job. Corey says, "Okay I will go Monday to look for a job."

"No. Today," she says. "But it is Saturday, who goes looking for a job on a Saturday? Corey rebuffs. She says...

"Okay, well... be the first person to get a job on a Saturday then. Until you go to college or get a job I will always be on you. All you want to do is play these damn video games, ever since you finished high school. I am telling you now Corey, the streets are not an option. The streets are always a dead-end road."

He responds with aggravation in his tone, "I have only been out of school for a month. It is not even July yet, and the first day of summer is a few days from here. You know what, never mind."

Corey is tired of his big sister preaching to him so just to shut her mouth he agrees to go look for a job today on a Saturday. Trina knows she rides him hard, but she feels like now it is her job to make sure Corey does not mess up his life.

Lou always stays out of the mix when Trina starts to preach to Corey. He does not say a word, because she does enough for the both of them.

Trina has been taking care of Corey since their parents died in a car accident ten years ago. Lou meet Trina about five to six months before the accident. Lou was always there for Trina when she was hurting the most from the loss of her parents. It always seemed like Lou was the friend she needed, as he helped Trina get back to her normal self. Their relationship has been strong ever since, as Lou continued to bond with Corey.

Trina always pretends she is angry, or acts as if it bothers her when Lou is bonding with Corey while playing video games late at night instead of being in bed with her.

But deep down inside she loves it. And Lou knows how much Corey means to her, so he puts in extra effort when it involves Trina and Corey's happiness.

Lou screams from the bedroom, "Where are my car keys?" "Did you check your pants pocket from last night?" Trina yells back. "Yes, I did! I have looked all over for them." Then Corey yells out, "Check the bathroom downstairs." The look on Lou's face says that he is not sure about that, so he says, "Why would they be in the bathroom downstairs?"

"Because you leave your keys all over the house," Trina says. Lou goes down stairs and checks the bathroom for his car keys. He yells, "I found them!" "Were they in the bathroom?" Trina asks. "Yes, they were, now come down here and give me a kiss before I go," Lou continues. Trina looks at Lou and says, "How about you give me a kiss for being right, as usual?"

Trina comes down the stairs to give Lou a five-second kiss before saying "Do not forget, I have to go to the store today." Lou leaves the house with a smile on his face

talking to himself, "that girl is
crazy."

Chapter 2

While walking to the car
Lou notices lots of dirt around his
rims and dust on the paint job. He
is confused, because the car is not
as he left it, but he does not pay
it too much mind... maybe just a dust
storm came through last night or
something. He gets into the car,
pulls out of his upscale home, then
drives off and goes to the hood to
make his rounds.

The first stop is his right-hand
man Ryder. Ryder runs everything in
the streets on Lou`s behalf. When
Lou was trying to get out of the
game like the rest of his crew,
Ryder asked Lou to show him how to
make money in the game without all
of the drama, the way that he did
it, and he will listen to everything
he says without question.

Lou did not want to do it at
first, but at the time a good friend
named Mego needed his help moving
over one hundred pounds of
marijuana, aka, "That Gas" at two
thousand dollars a pound.

Mego just stole it from some
duck ass niggas out in Cali after
they robbed three grow houses.
Mego's older sister told him the

perfect time and location to go take all of the weed that her boyfriend had just stolen. It was all because she caught him cheating on her.

Lou owed him big time, since Mego helped him get started when Lou and his crew were starving in these streets. Lou did not want to ask his crew to come back to help Mego, so he took Ryder up on his offer. It was only supposed to be for a few months, but in this game shit happens. Lou only would have done this favor for Ryder and only Ryder. He had some trust in Ryder, because he was the driver that Lou used whenever he and his crew had to go to Texas.

That is all of the driving Ryder did, but he always listened. The first thing Lou told Ryder is that when you are making money, drama finds you. It is all about how you handle your business.

The second thing is to trust no one outside of your circle. The deal Lou made with Ryder is that he will give him a pound of weed for twenty-five hundred a pound, but only if he gets it from him. If Lou finds out that he is making another move, their relationship will be over.

Ryder has a lot of respect for Lou. He had done so much for him so far, so why fuck it up now. Lou asks Ryder, "What is the word on the streets?" Ryder replies with, "They are about to have some big dogs from back in the day being released from prison."

Lou says, "Oh word," like nothing is wrong with that. So he asks Ryder who is being released and Ryder says, "I don't know their names yet, but I will find out later on for you though. Lou says, "No big deal. I have to go." Ryder says, "Leaving so soon?" "Yeah, I will be back Monday with the goods.

Ryder hands him a bag of cash, and Lou leaves. On to the second stop.

Chapter 3

Lou is having lunch with a business associate name Al G. Heat, but he just calls him Al. Lou does not trust him, but he needs him, and as long as Al needs Lou also, they get along well. So Lou arrives at the meeting an hour early to scope it out.

Lou orders some lunch at the bar before the meeting starts. He does not have time for bullshit talk just business, because he has one more stop to make before taking Trina to the store.

It is now 12:13 pm when Lou's food arrives, a Shrimp Po-boy dressed the way he likes it. He hurries to eat his lunch, so he can go back to the car and smoke a blunt before the meeting begins.

Lou is finishing his blunt when he sees Al pulling up, so he goes back inside of the restaurant to wait for Al there. Now high as a kite, Lou can not wait to get this meeting over and done.

Al keeps at least three guys with him, including the driver, who always stays with the car. Lou met Al through Mego at a party in Texas.

Mego owed Al $70,000 at the time, but first, he had to get one hundred thousand from Lou.

Mego met Lou at a Hotel on the south side of Houston. Took the money from Lou, counted out $30,000, and left the rest of it on the bed. Lou says, "You are not going to count the rest?" Mego says, "I did weigh the product, and I know it was about a hundred pounds." Lou says, "It was 115 pounds and a few ounces. The ounce is for me to smoke on."

Mego asks, "Did you sell out?" Lou replies, "No, I did not sell out. I still have over half of what you gave me left." "So what are you going to do when you run out of product?" Mego ask. "I do not know as of now, but things are moving slowly but surely," Lou says.

"Yes, slowly is correct, you and your crew would normally have that work gone in this time frame," Mego says. "Yep, you are right, but I am not doing this with them. Trell and Ronnie are out of the game. And I was too, until you ask me for this favor," Lou says.

Mego looks at Lou, and says, "Well I was going to this party, and if you care to join me, you can meet a few game changers and get well connected… unless you want out of the game?"

So that is how Lou met Al G. Heat.

Al and his two goons walk into the restaurant. They see Lou sitting down at the table where they meet four times a year, the first Saturday of the second month of each quarter at 1 pm. Lou stands up as Al and his two goons approach the table. He gives Al a nice firm handshake. Al says, "Hello Louis."

Al calls everyone by their real name. He does not do business with people who only go by their nickname. It is the first sign of disloyalty.

"Hey how are you doing?" Lou says to Al. "Hot! Can this city get any hotter?" Al laughs. Lou replies with, "Yes, it can."

The two sit down in their booth, across from Al's goons, sitting two tables over. "So, how is everything going Lou?" Fine, I have everything under control," Lou says. Al replies, "Well, I have some bad news. So first thing's first. Miguel is dead.

Lou says, "Miguel?" Lou looks puzzled. Al says, "Yes Miguel, Mego! Lou says, "Mego, man, what happened?" "A motorcycle accident. They say he was not wearing a helmet, but knowing Miguel he was drunk as fuck." Lou says, "Aw man."

Al says, "Wait, there is more bad news… this shipment is fifty pounds short, so I can not supply you with your product. At least not for the price we negotiated five years ago.

I will be getting it for the price that you are paying me as of now. That does not include shipping, and I have to still get it to you, right?"

Lou says, "So how much more are we talking about?" "Twenty-seven hundred per pound." Lou says, "If you can do $2,500 you have a deal."

Al says, "Ok then, we have a deal on the price. But I can not make any guarantees because I do not control the farm. I just know a guy, that knows a guy... my farm has been raided by the FBI, FDA, DEA, and the KKK I`m just saying I am hot Louis, and I am not talking about the weather or my good looks. I need your help moving some…"

Al, is interrupted by the waitress.

"Are you guys ready to order?" Lou says, "Not yet," and Al says, "I want a Coke, Louis do you want? A Coke, we will have two large Cokes." The waitress says, "Ok I will be back with your Cokes."

Al looks at Lou when the waitress is out of earshot, and says, "Did you get that?" Lou says, "Yes, and I kind of knew where you were going before you ordered two large Cokes." Al says, "But I wanted a sweet tea."

Lou laughs, "You are a fool dude." The two are still laughing, when the waitress comes back with the two Cokes, and Lou asks her, "Can I get a lemonade and a sweet tea also? The waitress says I hope y'all know what y'all want to eat. Y'all make ordering drinks a job." She leaves.

Al asks Lou, "So what's up, you in? Lou says, "I don't sell that shit, I never did, and I never will." Al replies, "Never say never. How do you think Miguel got started?

Miguel was a stickup kid and an opportunity came.

"He gambled with his life. You care to know how Miguel and I met?"

Lou pauses. Al looks Lou in the eyes, and decides to tell him.

"He robbed me, fled to New Orleans, and I guess that is how he met you. Then he came back with the cash to buy the same amount of marijuana I lost. So you know what I did Louis? I did nothing. I let him think he had gotten away with it.

I put a tail on him and followed him to New Orleans, and I said to myself this was my next move. I was looking to make moves to get my product to New Orleans. So I watched you and your crew grow. I only let Miguel live after I found out he stole from me, because he always came back to me if he needed more product. I never spoke on it to my crew.

Because it was a hunch, just putting two and two together. A guy I never heard of buying thirty pounds out of the blue. The same amount I lost. It made me dollars keeping you'll alive, and my reputation was not on the line. I

was going to kill Miguel and your
whole crew.

I not only wanted Miguel, but I
wanted everybody who was benefiting
from him robbing me. If he would
have gone any place in the world
besides New Orleans, I would have
done you'll in. So that is how I
feel about Miguel, I don't feel shit
for him. It is just business. And
that is what we have now, a business
relationship. Right?"

Lou says, "Right." "I asked
Miguel to bring you in so I can meet
the man who has been making me all
this money for all of these years.
You had your chance to walk away
from the game, and you didn't. You
didn`t have to come to my party.
Miguel was just the middleman to me.

Miguel is dead now. So if you
had not gone to my party, you would
be out of the game. So save that you
want out of the game bullshit. If I
did not tell you that Miguel was
dead, you would just be looking for
him, and all he would have done was
call me. I need your help moving
this work. So what is your answer?"
Al asks.

"Let me think about it," Lou
answers. Al retorts, "What is there

to think about?" Lou replies, "I need to find out who can help me move this shit. "Thin" niggas money is going to start getting low. If I am going to do it, I might have to take a few people out. It is like you asking me to start a war.

It is not like "The Gas". With that shit, I am on cruise control, because I put in my groundwork already."

Al says, "Ok then, think about it. I will be in town until Monday, and I need an answer by then. But take this into consideration when you are thinking about it.

If you need anyone hit, just let me know, and I will bring the added heat. You point them out, and I will take them out!!! Now I have to go. Call me before 5 pm with your answer, if you do not call, that means fuck me."

Lou says, "What is the number for the cola, twenty per key? I can piggyback the gas so it can be two thousand per pound instead of twenty-five hundred? I will be saving money on shipments." Al says,

"We can do that until you get tired of selling that cheap shit.

Call me." Al walks away with his goons.

The waitress comes back with the sweet tea and lemonade, and then she says, "Are you ready to order? Lou says, "No, just give me the check." She says, "Ok," and walks away.

Lou is drinking the sweet tea and lemonade, wondering what the fuck had just happened.

Chapter 4

Meanwhile, Ryder and his crew
are talking about their next moves.
Ryder asks his little brother Tank
to find out who is coming home from
prison. Tank is sixteen years old
and he sells coke behind his brother
Ryder back.

Three years ago Ryder asked Lou
about jumping into the cocaine game.
Lou shut it down. Lou told Ryder if
he felt like he made enough money in
the weed game, then do what he has
to do. He respected that Ryder came
to him first, so he will always have
Ryder's back, but he does not want
any part of that game. Ryder is the
only reason that Lou is still in the
streets. To Lou, Ryder saying that
he wants to go into the cocaine
game, is like saying he is out of
the weed game. His motto is do one
or the other.

Ryder says, "If I was to jump
into the coke game, what is the
first thing I will have to do?" Lou
replies, "The same thing you did in
the weed game, no different. Always
start small. Just because you have
the money to buy a brick, does not
mean you can sell a brick. Start
with a 2 and a ¼ that is all you

will need, and that is all Ryder
needed to hear.

He told Lou "Well I am not doing
it without you."

Lou says, "Good choice, that
game can change your life real fast
because of the amount of money you
make. But like my uncle told me, and
now I am telling you, the FEDS will
let you eat. Make all of the money
you want, until you start to kill
rivals or put out bad product that
is killing your customers. Do not
get their attention."

Tank asks Ryder, "Why do you
care who is getting out of prison?"
"I just want to know ok. Just
sometimes do what I say to do
please." Tank says" "Ok, ok,
anything else big bro sir yes sir."

Ryder says, "You always
playing."

Ok, all jokes aside, Ryder is
pissed off at his little brother yet
again, and his crew is laughing.
Ryder asks Money, Lil Duegie and,
Byron what they want to do, or
trying to do in the future? They all
respond with, what do you mean?

Ryder says, "I feel that there is more to life than just making money. I made so much money in the last three years...

...I have a house, cars, bitches; what's next? Dying or going to jail. We cannot do this for the rest of our lives, we have to think about going legal. I want to open a nightclub. So what about you'll? Do you guys have any other goals besides selling weed all day?"

Lil Duegie says, "This nigga going all Dr. Phil and shit. I am happy the way things are."

Byron says, "Me too, I am good," as he blows out a little smoke from the blunt he is puffing. Money says, "I feel you Ryder if they don't. I have a baby on the way. My girl told me last night."

Ryder says, "The next time I talk to Lou I will ask him how I get started on opening a night club." Tank chimes in, "You always asking that nigga what to do."

Ryder says, "He showed me how to do this step by step. Aren't we all eating, not in jail, and have no beef in the streets? That is because of him helping me. Do not expect loyalty if you are not loyal. The streets will eat you alive."

Tank says, "Did your boy Lou, tell you that too?" Ryder looks at Tank, and says, "Go, leave now, to do what I have already asked you to do about finding out who is getting released from prison."

Tank leaves the room and goes outside. Money asks, "Ryder what is all this about, you wanting to change. You want out the game?"

Ryder says, "No. My little brother looks up to me, but he does not listen. So I do not talk too much about serious business in front of him. He thinks I don't know it, but he is selling coke with Frank, or helping with Frank."

"How do you know?" Money asks? "Frank told me. At first he was trying to sell weed I told him no he was too young."

So Frank calls me six months ago like, your brother wants to work for me. So I told Frank to put him to work, but he does not listen. But, Frank says he has been listening to him, and everything he says to do. He is doing well. As long as he`s

working with Frank I will always
know what he is up too."

Ryder and Frank were close
friends before they started hustling
together they were "road dogs,"
everywhere Frank went Ryder went,
until Frank went to Juvenile
Detention for armed robbery. He was
arrested while hanging out with his
much older cousins and did a year in
Juvenile Detention.

Ryder and Money became real
cool, while Frank was in jail. Money
lives a few blocks up the road from
Ryder's house. They meet Lil Duegie
and Byron after Frank came home from
jail. Ryder knew Lou because he had
been driving up to Texas for him
once a month.

Then Lou started supplying Ryder
the marijuana that was mostly being
sold by Lil Duegie and Byron. They
were doing about a pound of weed a
week each, and purchasing it through
Money.

Money met them during a dice
game at his uncle's house, when he
overheard them talking about how
their weed connection had just
gotten murdered, and who they
thought had done it.

So he walked over to Lil Duegie
and Byron and asks, "Y'all smoke
weed?" "Fucking right!" Is their
reply. Money pulls out an ounce of
weed and says $200.
Byron says, "Smoke something!"
They roll up a few blunts and get
toasted. Byron bought the ounce from
Money that night, and they have been
making money together from that
point on.

In two years Byron and Lil
Duegie went from moving two pounds a
week to twenty pounds a week. Money
was making a killing on those two
alone. But he had three more guys he
was dealing with, rich white kids.

They earned him an added ten
pounds a week. Money is moving 30
pounds of weed a week. Making him a
profit of around $50-60,000 per
month. Frank started out moving an
ounce a day, by selling to crack
dealers and other hustlers that he
knew. They liked the weed Frank had,
so they paid his price. He was
making a killing at $400 per ounce
and making a profit of $3,900 per
pound he did ten pounds a month.
Selling 7 grams all day for a $100.

Ryder is making a profit of
$20,000 a month just dealing with
Lou and giving the work to Money and

Frank. Lou is making a killing doing nothing. He is getting one hundred pounds of marijuana for $1,500 each from Al. Lou charges Ryder $2,000 each. Lou profits $50,000 once a month. In two years Lou helped Ryder and his crew make a lot of money.

In that same time frame, Frank asks Ryder to jump into the coke game. But, it does not happen until Frank's cousin Tiger tells him about a new plug that he met while locked up. "We could make millions... and fuck the weed game. Did that done this, I am ready to grow," Frank says."Sounds like he is the man that can change your life," Ryder voices to Frank.

Coke is something Frank always wanted to do. Frank is ready. He did not ask many questions just, "How much for a brick?" Tiger says, "I don't know, I get a 9 piece, that is all I need. What, you have money for a Brick? Now I can find out how much it costs. How much money you have?" Frank says, "I have a $100,000 now."

Tiger replies, "Shiiit, bullshit… selling 7 grams for a $100. His cousin didn't believe him so Frank showed him. He made a phone call to his connection, once Frank showed him the money. He asked the number for a whole pie. The connect hangs up, and text back 30 on Tiger's phone.

Tiger tells Frank, thirty-three, and that he has to go in by himself... they do not like meeting new people, or some bullshit like that. You know, running game on Frank because he will be taking $3,000 per key off the top.

Frank loves and trust Tiger, so he immediately says cool, I want 3 of them. That`s when Frank told Ryder about his plan to jump into the Coke game.

Frank is very excited about the move. He cannot wait to see those bricks. It is like a milestone for him. "I am going to get three brick at $33,000 a peace you want one or two Ryder?" Franks ask. Ryder says, "I don`t know man not just yet. Let me talk to my big homie." Frank says, "We do this in two days." Ryder replies, "I will probably jump on the next boat. But do your thing. Be safe out there." That same night Ryder talked with Lou about jumping into the coke game. Turned out to be the same night Frank's cousin Tiger was robbed and murdered trying to buy 3 keys of coke. They got away with $90 grand that night, and Frank lost his first $100,000, and his first cousin, all in one night.

A week after Tiger`s funeral. Ryder was worried about Frank. Frank was twenty years old at the time. He already did time, lost a $100,000 and the death of Tiger was fucking his head up badly. So Ryder pulled up to Frank's house without calling.

He sees Frank outside loading a rental car. "What`s up dude?" Ryder says. Frank replies, "What are you doing here?" Ryder says, "Just checking on you. So what you up to, going somewhere?"

Frank says, "Well aren't you nosey, man we are going to ride on them fools who killed Tiger. Ryder says, "So y'all found out who did it then?" "Yep," Frank says. "I know that was not what you wanted to hear, but it is over for them, everybody getting hit up tonight. Ryder says, "Be careful, just call me when you get back in."

Frank interjects, "If you want to talk I have time now. I`m finish loading up the car so what`s up?" Ryder says, "Well you never came got your shit." Frank says, "You have it with you now?" Ryder answers, "Hell no. I am not stupid! That made me come check on you. You paid for ten pounds of gas and never came to pick it up."

Frank says, "I still have two pounds left from the last package." "What, are you quitting hustling now altogether?" Ryder replies, "No, I want to step it up… do both coke and weed. Tiger's bitch ass hid $9,000 in the trunk of his car."

Ryder looks confused. "Tiger's girl asked me to pick up his car from where he was robbed and killed. Chris drops me off and rolled out right away with his scared ass."

"So I am in the car driving, then I pull over to a carwash. I clean out evidence of other bitches and shit like that.

I pop the trunk, and in the same bag I put it in, I find my money, $9,000. He skimmed it off the top. His greed saved my life."

Ryder says, "Yep he would have wanted you there if he did not run game on you." Frank says, "All I have is $20,000, and twelve pounds of weed. I lost everything." Ryder says, "No you didn't lose everything, Tiger did. He`s dead. Frank do you remember when you made

your first $10,000 you thought you
were rich, and you only had two
pounds then. You just took a big
loss that's all."

Frank passionately replies to
Ryder, "I just don't know who to
trust. I keep on getting into fucked
up situations, why is that? I think
I am doing everything right, then,
boom!!! It is all gone in a blink of
an eye.
"I think I know what your
problem is... it is just what Lou
said to do. Grow your team. Stop
going at dudes that are already
doing it. To hell with niggas that
been in the game. Find niggas that
are trying to do it but need a
connection, and someone to help them
get on.

"Lou told me that when I first
started dealing weed for him. And
now it is you, Money, and I. We have
the weed game on lock now it is time
for the coke side to shake," Ryder
exclaims.

Frank says, "So you going in on
the coke game with me? Ryder says
"No, I can`t right now, but I am
there for you. I can give you the
game like Lou showed me. But if we
are going to do this, you cannot
sell both coke and weed. I will

handle the weed side and you deal
with the coke side ok. This also
means we cannot hang out with each
other in public. Only during private
get-togethers."

Frank asks, "Why can't we be
seen hanging out in public?"

"Because we are bosses now. We
don't hang out, we meet to talk
business and share information from
the other side of the fence. The
coke game is grimy, so if we are
going to play it the game starts
now. No one can know that we are
friends. I told Lou I was not going
to jump into the coke game," Ryder
says.

Frank asks, "Why did you tell
him that?" Ryder says, "He was going
to stop bringing in the gas. So I
said I will chill on that issue. But
Lou does not know you so we are
good. You were in jail when Lou and
I hooked up."

"So what is the first thing to
do? How do I put a team together?"
Frank asks.

"Your team is going to come to
you. I wondered the same thing. But
I do know, that you are either
coming up or falling off, bottom

line. You came up in the weed game. You took a big loss in the coke game. You have $20,000 left and now it is time to come back up," Ryder replies.

"You are right, and it is time for a few niggas to fall off," Frank says. Ryder asks Frank, "Do you have a connect?" "The dude Tiger normally got his work from his name is To Too."

"Is he cool to deal with?" Says Ryder. "Hell yeah, and he came to Tiger's funeral and everything, Frank exudes.

Ryder says, "Ok, we can start with him but do not buy anything more than two and a quarter. Always keep it small when you start scoring dope. Get your clientele up first and find some hitters who you can trust. The streets do not pay for anything it can take for free, so as long as you are doing what I said to do, your team will come to you."

"Did you come to me to put you on?" Ryder continues. Frank replies, "Right, right."

That is how Frank and Ryder became partners in the coke game. Frank was tired of everything going wrong so he listens to Ryder's every word.

Byron walks into the room and yells out, "Is the food ready yet?" Ryder replies, "I think there are some hot dogs and chips ready, but the beans, mac and cheese, nope." Byron walks out of the room to go get something to eat.

Lil Duegie tells Money, "So you are having a baby huh boy!" Ryder says, "Congratulations. I didn't know that." "Thanks fellas," Money says.

Lil Duegie says, "You thought Ryder wanted out of the game? He played that card quickly. I'm having a baby." Ryder laughing Lil Duegie says jokingly, "He said she told him last night, but she told him before he left the house today. I am having a baby."

Ryder says, "But I really do want a night club." He looks over to Money, "We can start one together, me and you, book concerts and shit to clean our money up. You can run the legal business, since you are having a baby and all."

Lil Duegie says, "It sounds to me like y'all have had enough to drink. I am just getting started."

Meanwhile, Tank is on his way to meet with Frank. He gets a phone call from Bam, he need a ride to pick up his car from the body shop. Tank says ok, but he has to do it right now because he has to go meet with Frank.

Bam says, "I will ride with you then, I have to see him also." Tank says, "Ok, I will be there in fifteen minutes.

Tank arrives at Bam's house. He calls Bam and tells him that he is outside, but Bam asks him to come inside because he is still getting ready.

"You told me fifteen minutes, and you here in seven minutes," Tank says. "Man just hurry up, I will wait in the car," Tank says. "Ok I will be out in five minutes," Bam says.

Tank gets on Instagram while waiting for Bam to get ready. Bam is inside trying to find his car keys before he realized his key is at the body shop. He starts talking to himself, "I need to stop smoking."

He leaves the house and gets into the car with Tank who is still on Instagram. Bam asked in a crazy tone, "You ready nigga?" Tank says, "Don`t rush me." Bam replies, "You not fucking with one of them bitches. Are you even fucking yet?" Tank says, "Nigga you know I`m fucking, don`t even play with me about fucking like that." "Like what dude?" "Man, let's go." They pull off continuing to argue about their sex lives.

Chapter 5

Meanwhile, Lou pulls up at his uncle Bowe house. His uncle Bowe is the reason Lou is where he is at today. He gives Lou solid advice when he is confused about what to do in life. Lou walks inside the home to find his uncle Bowe sitting in his favorite chair smoking the best cigar money can buy.

"What up unc'?" Lou asks. "Nothing much, hanging in there nephew, how is my sister doing?" Mom, she doing good I`m going over there tomorrow to check in on her," Lou replies.

Lou asks his uncle if he is home alone. Uncle Bowe explains that for now Mary and the grandkids or out doing some shopping and they will be back in a couple of hours. "I gave her three thousand dollars cash, she flew out of here, Bowe says. Lou chuckles, "Man, so that is how you got some free time."

Bowe proclaims, "She is happy, I am happy the grandkids are happy, and it only cost me $3,000." Lou says, "If I give my girl money, then I have to drive her to the store, ooh! Speaking of that, we are going to the store later. She is going to start blowing my phone up if I am not back home in the next hour or two."

Bowe says, "Women you got to love them. So what is going on nephew? What is the word on the streets?" Lou says, "Well, it is a long story." Bowe says, "I love long stories."

Lou says, "To make a long story short, the nigga I am getting my work from wants me to graduate to powder. You know I don`t fuck with that shit unc', and he wants an answer by 5 pm on Monday." Bowe replies, "Well neph', don`t fuck with it!"

Lou says, "I wish it was that simple. I think he killed Mego." "Mego, that is the kid from Texas right? Bowe asks. "Yeah."

Bowe inquires, "Why do you think he kill Mego?"

Lou says, "Because he did not need Mego anymore, and we robbed him when we first started in the game. I do not know if he knows for sure, or if he thinks we had something to do with robbing him. But the way he is putting on is that he thinks it was Mego by himself. That is how I meet him, through Mego, and he told me Mego was dead right before I came here. For all I know Mego is still alive."

Bowe pauses for a moment before saying, "So let me get this straight, the nigga you getting work from in this present day and time, you robbed him back in the day, but you don't know if he knows?"

"Right," and he wants an answer by Monday before 5 pm," Lou answers.

Bowe asks, "What are the terms and conditions?"

Lou says, "Twenty grand a key and he is willing to take out the competition. I just have to set shit up.
Bowe says, "Well nephew it seems to me this nigga means business, that is a deal you best not refuse. You have some damn good numbers and he is going to help you get started. And I am sure he knows you are going to need some time to get going. Who is this nigga anyway?"

Lou responds with, "Al G Heat."
"He sounds like a singer. I am going to make a call, and see if I can dig up some shit up on him. Al G Heat

huh?" Lou asks, "So what should I do?"

Bowe says, "I would call him before 5 pm Monday. Tell him yes and sound excited when you call him." Lou replies, "I had a feeling you were going to say that." "I am only telling you to say yes, to buy us more time to shake him off your back one way or another. So play by his rules for now," Bowe rebuts.

Arf-arf, arf-arf, arf-arf. It is Bowe`s dog, a Chihuahua named Ta Ta. Bowe says, "Someone must be pulling up in front of my house."

Lou gets up to check it out. He looks out of the window he sees a truck with lawn equipment on it. Lou says, "Are you getting your grass cut today?" "Oh that is Johnny, green truck?" Bowe asks.

Lou says, "Yeah it is a green truck. Thanks again for the advice. I am going to run to the barbershop, and get my car washed while it is still early." "Ok then, be safe Neph'."

Chapter 6

Tank and Bam are on the way to the workhouse. At the same time, Frank is texting Tank to let him know that he has to make a run, and will be back in an hour, and that he put everything in the safe.

Frank leaves the workhouse, walks to his car. As he is getting in BANG BANG! BANG! BANG! BANG! BANG! BANG! All shots were to the back of Frank's head. He never saw it coming.

The neighbors are now looking out of their windows. Some are calling 911. Then, two minutes later, Tank and Bam arrive pulling up next to Frank's car. The two get out of the car, and walk to the other side of Frank's car to find him halfway in his car shot dead.

Tank and Bam see Frank's brain matter, blood, and fluids splattered all over the car. They scream in horror, "Aaah! Aaah! What the fuck is going on!" The yell, as they try to digest what they see.

The whole scene is enough to cause Bam to start throwing up. How can someone overcome the shock of seeing something like that, so up close and so personal?

The neighbors are now starting to come outside. Tank is crying like a baby over his best friend Frank. Frank was like an older big brother, but cooler than Ryder.

Tank takes his phone out to call Ryder, when he notices the text that Frank sent him earlier. He continues his call to Ryder, but he does not answer. So he continues up the front steps of the workhouse, and unlocks the door with no weapon in his hand before walking through the front door.

Tank steps forward into the house slowly, kind of scared, and a little nervous when his phone rings. It is Ryder calling him back. Tank answers the phone panicked, "Big Bro they killed Frank!" Ryder is not sure what he just heard, so he screams, "What!!!?" "Tank they killed him! They killed him, just now, right before we pulled up. They killed him, man," as he is fighting back tears hearing Ryder's familiar and oddly comforting voice.

Ryder says to Tank, "Man the fuck up, and talk to me nigga. What-the-fuck is going on?" Tank exudes,

"Nigga, Frank is dead!" Ryder says, "They killed Frank." "Yes, yes nigga that's what I'm trying to tell you, they killed him right before we pulled up," Tank says, as he continues to fight back his tears, as if it were some form of bravado to show Ryder he is actually "Manning Up".

Ryder says, "What do you mean we? Who are you with?"

"Bam, you do not know him. Ryder says, "You with them random-ass niggas." Tank responds, "Not now with this." Ryder says, "Are the cops there yet Tank?" "No." "Where did it happen?" Tank says, "I guess he was getting into his car." Ryder asks, "Where are you at now, inside the workhouse? "Yes." "Hurry up and grab all of the shit before the cops come. It will make Frank seem like a bad dude, and get the fuck from around there."

Tank does what Ryder says to do, and as they are pulling off, the cops are starting to arrive. That was way too close for comfort, although it did allow them to focus on something besides the sight of Frank's dead body, if not for a few moments.

Ryder is outside of the house away from everyone. He has yet to tell Money the bad news. Byron and Lil Duegie are not as close to Frank like Ryder and Money, but they still know him. Ryder decides to call Franks cousin Toya. They use to mess around as kids.

Toya answers the phone, "You miss me baby." Ryder says, "You must not know then, you are too cheerful." Toya says, "Boy, what are you talking about?" "Someone killed Frank today, about 30 minutes ago." "What?!" Toya screams. Ryder tells her, "Let the rest of the family know, and I do miss you. I have to go now. Sorry to be the barer of bad news. I will text you the address where it happened... are you there?"

Toya dropped the phone to the ground as Ryder was still talking. She is devastated, curled in a ball on the floor, and sobbing uncontrollably.

Money comes outside and sees Ryder looking pissed the fuck off, eyes bloodshot red. Money says, What's up homie you good? Ryder says, "Someone just killed Frank." Money responds, "Damn, fuck!"

He steps away from Ryder to try
to gather himself, but his grief is
deep, and quickly manifests into
anger, as he and Money leave to
ponder their next moves.

Chapter 7

Lou pulls up to the car wash and right across the street is the barbershop. He leaves his key with the kids so they can move the car when it is finished. Then he walks to the barbershop.

They are only three chairs inside of the barbershop, as Lou walks in, he sees his Barber finishing up with a customer. Lou says, "What is going on everyone? I guess I am right on time." His Barber replies, "You mean right on the money. Sit down before my lunch comes, or you will be waiting until after I eat."

Lou hurries to the chair and sits down. He says, "I know you mean it. It would not be the first time you did me that." "And it is probably not going to be the last time if you keep coming on my lunch break," his Barber says. "I hate warming up food. I love my food freshly hot. Just last week I stop cutting Joe's hair to eat my food," the Barber continues.

Lou laughs and replies, "Man you are crazy." The Barber says, "Not crazy, just hungry! And you may be my next victim, just let my food

come, you'll see what I mean."
Everyone in the barbershop goes into
an uproar of laughter.

Just then, Lou's cell phone
rings, and it is Trina. "What's up
babe?" He says. "Nothing just a
reminder about taking me to the
store." "Don't worry, I didn't
forget, I will be there after I
leave the barbershop." "That is all
I wanted to know, I love you, and be
careful," she says. Lou says, "I
love you too," as they hung up the
phone.

The barber says to Lou, "I know
one thing, you better hope my food
don`t come."

Lou says to his Barber, "Every
since the car crash she has been
afraid to drive. She has a driver's
license and all. And, on top of
that, her brother wrecked the car we
got him, now she is fearing for his
safety."

The Barber says, "It seems like
she is taking the death of her
parents extra hard. Only time can
help her with that. You just keep
being there for her that's all. She
seems like a good young lady, and
you'll work well together."

"Yeah, she really is a good
girl," Lou says.

Chapter 8

Tank and Bam are in the car driving, on the way to see Ryder. Bam is talking to Tank, but Tank's mind is off somewhere else he is into deep thought, and he is not speaking a word.

Seeing his friend dead next to his car and his big brother Ryder on the phone telling him to man the fuck up. Tank feels like he did not handle his business like he was supposed to. Tank had never seen a dead body before, and the first dead body he sees on the streets was his friend Frank.

He is pissed that he froze up like a coward, and he thinks to himself; what would I have done if my brother had not called me back when he did, I can't believe that I was so scared. I will never show fear again.

I promise you that! Tank makes a deal with himself, and then snaps out his daze. Bam is still shaken up as well. Bam asks Tank, "Who was Frank beefing with?" Tank says, "Nobody, we were eating good, that is all I can see."

Bam says, "But they didn't rob him." "I know, but now he is out the game, and dead," says Tank. Bam replies, "So what do we do now?" Tank, "I don't know yet."

"Yo' you passed the turn!" Bam shouts. Tank says, "What are you talking about." "You have to take me to get my car, remember?" "Oh, I did, I forgot," Tank says. "When you get your car, come to my house, I have to meet with my brother," he adds.

"You still need to re-up on product?" Tank asks. "That is why I was riding with you in the first place," Bam says. Tank drops Bam off at the body shop, and goes straight home to meet with Ryder.

Lou leaves the barbershop with a fresh haircut and a clean car. He is on his way home to take Trina to the store. When he walks inside, he sees Corey playing his play station and Trina is upstairs on the phone.

Lou yells at her to see if she is ready, but Trina tells him she has to take another shower since she just finished her workout. Lou says to himself, "Really?" Trina yells, "I am not going to be long." Corey says to Lou, "Want to get in a game of Madden right quick. I still owe you an ass-kicking." Lou says, "Start it up."

"Man, I cannot believe she called me over an hour ago to take her to the store. She is not just not ready, but she never even started getting ready." Corey says, "I guess you do love her, you put up with a lot," I would have left her crazy ass."

Lou says, "Nigga you just mad she ride your ass so hard. But the crazy part is, all women do it, you can't run from them getting dressed on their own time, holding purses and bags in the mall. All that crazy shit. That is why the play station was invented, to kill time and not your woman." They both laugh playing the game while Trina is getting ready.

In the middle of the 4th quarter of the game, Trina comes downstairs, "I am ready," she says. Lou replies, "Of course. Babe, just give me five minutes," he says.

Now Trina is rushing Lou off the game when the score is tied up with two minutes left in the 4th quarter, Lou has the ball on the thirty-yard line, and Trina says, "That is all y'all do…"

Lou and Corey finish up their game. Lou snaps the ball Corey intercepts, and returns it for a touchdown, and Lou gives up on the game when he sees that certain look on Trina's face.

She says, "What!" Lou just laughs, "You ready?" Trina says, "Yes, and it is not my fault you lose again." Lou replies, "I didn't say it was." Trina says, "But you were thinking it." "Really? Let's go," Lou rebuts.

Corey yells out, "I'll give you a rematch when you get back." Trina replies, "Get a job," as they walk out the door.

Now at the store for over two hours, Lou's phone starts to ring repeatedly. Different numbers are calling, and most are unknown, but he is still not answering his phone. Whoever is on the other line is not more important then Trina. While in the check out line, Trina's phone rings. It is her girlfriend Lora.

Trina answers, and Lora says, "Girl where you at? I am at the store, why what is up?" "I have some bad news." Trina says, "What is it?" Trina looks confused. Lora answers, "Someone has just killed Lou, right outside of Bizzy Bee's store. They shot up his car."

Trina replies, "That has to be someone else. My man is right here with me. Lora says, "Really, well I am out here now, and I see his car with thirty are more bullet holes." Trina says, "Look, let me call you back."

They hang up and Trina tells Lou what Lora just said, and Lou jokingly tells her that she needs to get new friends.

Trina and Lou are walking out the store laughing and joking about what Lora said, when Lou asks Trina, "Where did we park?" Trina thought they parked where they were standing, and so did Lou. Trina says, "Let's just look around before we report the car stolen, it may just be lost in this big ass parking lot."

Lou says, "Were did Lora say she was at? In our old hood,by Bizzy Bee`s." They continue to look around for the car and Lou's phone rings it is Jason.

Lou answers the phone, this time because of what is going on. "Man, I thought you were dead! Niggas calling my phone saying your car just got shot up and shit." Lou says,"My girl just told me her friend just called her and said the same shit.

Jason asks, "What the fuck is going on?" Lou replies "Well, right now, I am in the store parking lot with over three hundred dollars worth of food and party items in the shopping cart looking for my car. Now I am thinking that someone stole my car."

Jason says, So niggas might not be lying about seeing your car shot up. Lou says, "You think it is my car." "That is the word on the streets." "Ok, if I am dead, let's keep me dead. Do not tell anyone you spoke to me. I will call my family myself. I have to play my cards right, let me call you back," Lou says.

Trina says, "We need to call the police." Lou replies, "We do but not now, let me call Ronnie, we need to get home first." Lou calls his good friend Ronnie and he answer.

Ronnie answers the call with, "Man I am glad to hear your voice I just got a call saying you had been killed." Lou says, "Well, that's the rumor. I called because I need a favor. I need a ride home. Somebody stole my car, I am on Bullard Road at the superstore."

Ronnie says, "I am not too far from you, I will be there in 10 minutes." They hang up, and like he said within 10 minutes Ronnie pulls up.

Chapter 9

Ryder is outside talking to Tank, Lil Duegie, Byron and Money about Frank's death, as family and friends start to arrive at the party for Ryder's baby sister Raven, who turned five years old.

Ryder's cell phone rings, and it is an unknown caller. Ryder answers the phone, "Hello." "What up man! This Tyson." Tyson, is Frank`s big cousin Tyson, known for knocking fools out, and will take your life just as fast.

"Toya gave me your number. She said you was out there when it happened, and I`m trying to find out what is going on."

Ryder says, "Toya must have heard wrong. I was not there, no one was." Tyson says, "Then how you know Frank was dead?" "My little brother found him dead, called me, and I called Toya to tell her to let you all know what happened," Ryder says.

Tyson asks, "Tank is your little brother right?" Ryder says, "Yeah."

Tyson says, "I met him a few times, and Frank was showing him a lot of love. I know you all did not have anything to do with Frank's death. We kind of already know what is going on, we at war with them niggas who kill Tiger, and we road on them, now they rolling back on us, so now they know we are coming, and they are ready for us too. It is what it is."

Ryder asks, "So you'll know that for sure. Tyson replies, "Well not really, do you know something I should know about Frank's death?" "Frank had no beef's that I know of. My little brother would have known," Ryder adds.

Tyson says, "Well, maybe it was a robbery the safe was open, and the door was open to the apartment. Frank had just re-upped on that white girl. It is all gone, money and all, if he did not get robbed."

Ryder knows Tyson is fishing for the unsold drugs and money Frank had in the safe. But what he does not know is Ryder, was Frank's partner, so what is missing belongs to Ryder and Tank now.

Tyson feels like that is my family's product, and if you have it give it up.

Tyson says, "I was talking to the nigga we get our work from he told me how much Frank just picked up sooo."

Ryder asks, "So what are you trying to say, I robbed Frank?" Tyson replies, "You did not Rob or kill Frank, but your brother has the work, and the cash and I want it back. The neighbors saw the kid who always be at Frank`s apartment leave with a black duffle bag. They also said they pulled up after the gunshots, screaming, throwing up, and shit, so I know you'll didn't kill my cousin."

Ryder says, "Well I will talk to him when he comes back. Let me found out what is going on and I will call you back off the same number." Tyson replies, "You do that," and they hang up the phone.

Everyone who is outside on the porch heard the way Ryder responded to the questions, and are wondering what is going on. Ryder explains that was Frank`s cousin Tyson, and he wanted him to give all of the money and dope back.

Tank is the first to respond. "Fuck him! Frank did not trust him anyway." Byron says, "How the fuck he want to ask for something. He put nothing on. You and Frank were partners."

Ryder says, "But he does not know that." Tank chimes in, "What kind of partners were you'll? "Lets just say I know everything you been up to while working with Frank." Lil Duegie says, "Man! I would have just told that nigga what it is. It is my shit, Frank and I were partners, and this is my shit."

Money says, "Right, for real Ryder. You should have shut that shit down."

Ryder says, "That nigga would not have believed me, he thinks that Frank tells him everything, and if I would have said we were partners and he still demanded I give him all of the work and money… we would be at war tonight with them niggas. I will have to hit first, so that is why I did not tell him anything."

Tank says, "Fuck him, lets go." Tank pulls out his gun. Lil Duegie says, "What you know about slinging that iron?" And Tank replies, "I saw what it did to Frank. If they can pull it without giving a fuck, so can I. Like I said fuck him." Money says, "Sound like you are ready, but who is that nigga pulling up.

Everyone looks toward the unknown car, and Tank says, "That is Bam." "Who!" Said almost everyone on the porch. The dude I was with when I went by Frank. We were working together with Frank. He went to the hood spots, and I went to the good neighborhoods. We know all of Frank's people.

He looks over at Ryder, "He is coming to re-up he called when you were on the phone with Tyson," Tank says

Ryder asks, "So how much he coming to get." Tank says, "Now that, I don't know." Ryder says, "So how much is in the bag?" "A brick in a half," Tank answers. Ryder says, "Give him a two and a quarter. That is all! I do not care what he said Frank was giving him. I know a two and a quarter should keep him good for tonight. I have to still find out how I am going to handle Tyson. You go inside and deal with your friend. You are lucky that is Frank's boy." Tank answers,

"Who died and made you in charge?" Tanks asks. Ryder says, "You want me to kick your ass."

Everyone laughs at the two brothers,
as Bam is walking up to the house.

Chapter 10

Tank introduces Bam to the crew. Ryder and his crew had very little words to say. Tank and Bam go inside to conduct business while everyone else stays outside.

Tank is looking for the Duffle bag that is sitting right next to Bam. Bam says, "What are you looking for?" Tank says, "The black duffle bag." "This one right here?" Bam asks. Tank replies "I am tripping I looked right at it." Bam says, "Still fucked up behind seeing Frank like that Huh?" Tank says, "It is that plus Tyson wants all of the work back."

Bam asks, "What you talking about? I am confused." Tank explains, "Everything in the duffle bag, that nigga want it because it belongs to Frank." Bam asks, "So we will be working for him now?" Tank replies, "No man, let me finish talking. You see, my brother and Frank are very close. I mean, were very close… they were partners. That is how I ended up working with Frank. I just found this out, but no one else knew that, but them."

Bam says, "A dead man can`t confirm that, for all I know your brother could have been making it all up. Brother or not in this game I was taught this is a dog eat dog game. Trust no one at any given moment. Situations can change in a heartbeat or whenever a heart stops beating. Tank says, "My brother has no reason to lie, and I trust him with my life."

Bam says, "I am not saying not to trust your brother, it is just hard to believe from my point of view.

Tank screams out, "B.I.N.G.O! That's the problem… my brother did not tell Tyson yet because Tyson would not believe him, Tyson thinks I have the work, and my brother told him I did not come home yet. So he brought a little time to come up with something. Tyson does not know he is asking for my brother`s dope. And if you do not believe it, then Tyson wont."

Bam says, "You could be telling the truth, but it is hard to believe. Tyson is crazy he will say all is good the same day he has you leaking from somewhere." Tank says, "It is either give it to him, or go to war. That is how my brother must be feeling. He might be on the phone with Lou right now."

"What? Lou the old O.G?" Bam
asks. Tank says, "Lou is an O.G.?"
Bam says, "Was an O.G. He was killed
earlier today. His car got shot the
fuck up." Tank looks at him in
disbelief. "Really, it just happen I
think about two hours ago," he
continues. Tank asks, "Are you sure
we talking about the same Lou?" Bam
replies, "Only one O.G. I know name
Lou." Tank says, "I am not going to
say nothing to him just yet, since
we just lost Frank.

Bam says, "I have to get going I
have money to make and bills to pay.
Tank says "Here is a two and a
quarter. You don`t have to pay back
shit, just re-up with us. Bam says,
"This shit will be gone before
midnight." Tank replies, "Frank
never stepped on it, so be careful
cutting that shit. Do not add to
much soda trying to be greedy." Bam
says, "I got this, I will see you
tomorrow."

Tank walks Bam outside, as Ryder
and his crew are still discussing
what happening. Bam say`s his good
bye's to everyone, get`s in his car,
and drives off.

Chapter 11

Lou and Ronnie are dropping off Trina to put away all the items they purchased for the party. Also, to pack some cloths for a week, Lou does not know what is really going on right now, so he wants to keep his family safe for right now. He tells Trina to be ready by the time he gets back. They are sleeping at a hotel for the night.

"Make sure you tell Corey to pack also he is coming too," Lou adds. Trina says, "So I guess this is not a romantic get away." Lou says, "It may turn into one. I will be back in an hour or less. I am going to check out the crime scene." Lou kisses Trina and walks out the door.

Ronnie is in the car already, wondering what the hell is going on. Lou gets in the car. Ronnie looks at Lou and says, "Are you in any beef I should know about?" "No, I am trying to find out what is going on myself," Lou says.

Ronnie and Lou pull up to the crime scene. They park but do not get out of the car. They did not need to. Lou saw what he needed to see. Lou sees his car shot up and looking like Swiss cheese.

He can tell the windows were up because of all the glass. Ronnie makes the comment that, "Whoever shot up your car, was not trying to miss." Lou says, "Somebody wants me dead, my windows are too dark to see in there, they wanted me dead, and they did not give a fuck who was with me."

Ronnie asks, "So what is next?" Lou replies, "I need a car. I guess I will be renting a car tonight or tomorrow. Ronnie says, "My daughter is punished, you can use her car. It is a Chevy Malibu."

Lou says, "I just need it for a day or two. I am going to still need to rent a car. For now, I need to get back home." Ronnie and Lou pull off, heading away from the crime scene to go to Ronnie's house.

Right now Lou's main concern is to get Trina and Corey to a safer place. Ronnie pulls up to his upper class home, and gives Lou the keys to his daughter's car. Lou leaves right away. He pulls up to his house fifteen minuets later, to find Trina and Corey still putting up all the newly purchase items.

They never started to pack and Lou is pissed. Lou yells, "What are you'll doing? Why are you'll not packing?" Trina replies, "What makes you think we are not packed already?"

Lou asks, "Well, are you? Trina replies, "Yes, we are just putting up the food items. I do not want my meat to go bad." Lou humbles himself, "Ok then, finish up. Corey and I will load up the car, so hurry up," Lou says. Trina asks, "Where are we going?" Lou replies, "Biloxi, Mississippi."

Corey says, "I am going to the beach." Lou replies, "This is not a vacation. We are laying low until I find out what is going on."

As he and Corey walk out the door Lou gets a text from Ryder that reads: "I need to talk to you" Lou does not respond, and feels that the word has not traveled that far, since Ryder is of the frame of mind that Lou is still alive. Lou wants to keep it that way, and let him find out from the streets that he has been murdered.

Lou and Corey pack up the car, and Trina walks out to join them, before take off on their trip to Biloxi. Once they are on the road Trina asks Lou, "What all do you know as of now?"

He replies, "Well your friend was right, she did see my car in the hood shot up looking like Swiss cheese. But who was inside of the car, I do not know. So once I get you'll to safety I will call my lawyer.

Cory says, "Why do you need your lawyer, you did not do anything wrong." Lou smiles at Corey through the rear view mirror and says, "Go to a nice school." Corey asks, "What is that suppose to mean?

Lou replies, "Corey, life is chess not checkers. This is my situation, facts; my car has been stolen while your sister and I were shopping, we did not call the police right away, and as of now, at all. Now, my car is a crime scene and once they check the vin number on the car, they will know everything they need to know about the person who owns the car which is me. They will have a lot of questions to ask me, so that is why I must go in with my lawyer," he says.

"In turn, I will be trying to find out who wants me dead, my car window was tinted, so who ever shot my car up, will still try to kill me once they find out that was not me they murdered. Or they may go into hiding, you never know, so always assume the worst when at war. I am not running from the cops I am repositioning myself to fight back without getting hurt or killed. I do not know who wants me dead but all I know is, they made their first attempt," he concludes.

Chapter 12

Ryder and his crew are still outside of the house on the front porch. Tank sees his brother looking worried on how he should handle Tyson. "Ah, big bro I have some bad news," Tank says out of the blue.

Ryder gives him a what are talking about now look. Tank continues, "Lou is not going to text you back." Ryder replies, "And you know this how?" Tank says, "Bam told me before he left, that some O.G. named Lou was killed today in his car. I wasn't going to tell you tonight because you are already dealing with Frank's death. But since you are waiting on Lou to call you back, I had to say something."

Ryder says, "That is some bullshit, people are always spreading rumors." Money asks, "Where did it happen?" "I don't know, but I can find out," Tank says. Ryder says, "I would find out right now what is going on."

Tank text Bam, "Where did you say Lou was killed?" Ryder makes a call to find out if Tank's statement is true.

Bam texts back, "In the hood by the Down Home store." Tank says, "Bam just texted me back. He said Lou was killed in the hood by the Down Home store." Ryder says, "I am going to check this out, I must see for myself." Money says, "I will roll with you."

Byron says, "Well I have to head out, my people are getting low on work, so just call me and let me know the next move." Lil Duegie says, "I am in the same boat I have to leave also. So if your boy is dead Ryder, how you are going to handle Tyson knowing how that nigga is." Ryder says, "I will cross that bridge when I get to it, but first I must confirm whether or not Lou is dead." Tank responds with, "All that is cool, but what if it is true, what are you willing to do because giving back the work is not an option?"

"Tank is right, Lil Duegie chimes in. "Just hit him up do not call him… sneak attack before they think you had something to do with it. Tyson doesn't have any beef with you as of now. Once you find out or not Lou is dead that should be your next move," he adds.

Tank says, "Frank always said that Tyson's number was coming, because he is caught up in too much beef and bullshit. So if we steal a car, and mask up, we should get away with it. Byron says, "We out, call me when you'll get back. Tank goes inside and everyone else leaves.

Lou checks his family into a hotel in Biloxi, Mississippi. Trina is scared with a mix of emotions and don`t know if Lou is going to jail or going to die. All she wants is for it to be all over with and Lou is safe at home with her.

Lou and Corey are unloading the car. Corey asks Lou, "What can I do to help?" Lou says, "Nothing but look after your sister and stay strong for her. I have to leave and go back to New Orleans. While I am gone stay off social media, and do not call anyone, or me for that matter, I will call you guys ok!

Lou and Corey finish unloading the car, while Trina is in the hotel room lying across the bed when the two of them return. Lou explains what he told Corey, so now he is telling Trina the same thing about staying off the phones and social media.

Trina says, "So you just want us to stay here and hope you call. You acting like the CIA are after you." Lou says, "So you think I`m going over-board." Trina replies, "Yes and no."
Lou tries to comfort Trina. "Now what is that suppose to mean, everything will be fine," he says.

Trina says, "Well you are being paranoid, but you got us to a safe spot. So I have no problem with that. We have money, and we are good for few months. But now you just want us to wait? What if you go to jail or get killed, how am I suppose to know what to do or think if you don`t call me?"

Lou replies, "I am not going to die and I am not going to jail." She sarcastically says, "So we came to Biloxi for nothing then right?"

Lou knows that she is right, but he is not going to admit this one so he changes the subject. "Look, I have to call Raymond if anything would happen to me, you call him no one else. I will text the number to you. Trina says, "Who is he?" Lou replies, "Raymond is my Lawyer."

Lou leaves the hotel room, gets into his car, and heads back to New

Orleans. Now he is ready to face the world. The first thing he does is call Raymond. Raymond answers the phone, and Lou says to him, "I need you big time, I don`t know what the hell is going on." Raymond says, "Well hello to you to Louis." "My bad, I have a lot going on right now," Louis replies. Raymond rebuts, "I know, it is all over the news. I was expecting your phone call." "Really! I mean what are they saying."

Raymond tells him the reports about Lou being killed in his car along with another person. Then, about the conflicting reports, that Lou may be responsible for the murder of the two teens that stole the car.

"Man that did not happen, nothing like that. Can we meet tonight? Raymond says, "Yes we can." "Meet me in our same spot," Raymond requests. Lou asks Raymond to give him about an hour, since he was on the road heading back to the city.

Ryder and Money are at the crime scene looking at Lou`s car, as it is being lifted onto the back of a tow truck. Money blurts out, "This is either, a new beginning, or the end of our run. "I don`t get it," Ryder says.

Money explains, "Lou is our plug. Plus, Tyson wants your work, and even then, how are we going to re up on the weed?" Ryder says, "I'll think of something, but what I am not going to do is fold under pressure.

My big homie always said when you are making money, drama finds you. It is how you deal with it that`s all. Money says, "Lets get out of here. Ryder gives in to his motions and proclaims, "What a day, dog eat dog world, you are either built for it, or not. You either want it, or you don`t. These niggas kill two of my dudes in the same day. Man I can`t believe this sh#t! Fu@k!

Everything that is going on hits Ryder all at one time. He really does not know what to do, besides remember what Lou taught him. It is time for one of those lessons to be put to good use. First thing's first. Lou told him, never make decisions based on emotions. Always think of what is the best move to grow, without getting killed or going to jail.

Money asks Ryder, "Where are we going." Ryder looks at him while driving and says, "What you have to go home?" Money says, "No man. You don`t realize you made the block we back were we started. Look I know you hurting Ryder. But,nigga, speak! So now what?"

Ryder replies, "Let go to "The Truck Stop", have a few drinks, and keep our ears open. Let's see what the word is on the streets."

The Truck Stop is their favorite watering hole to have a few drinks.

Chapter 13

Al G Heat is calling Lou`s cell phone after watching the news. He is just as confused as everyone else, but Lou is not answering the phone. At this stage, everyone has a lot of questions, with not a lot of answers.

Tyson is calling Ryder`s cell phone, and Ryder is not answering. Tyson hangs up the phone, but now he is starting to look a little pissed. He is wondering if Ryder is playing games with him, or up to something else. He is not ready to make a move on Ryder, as of now, because it is still early. But he likes instant results.

Lou calls Raymond to let him know that he will be there in five minutes. Raymond lets Lou know that he is already there, as he is just pulling into a parking spot.

Raymond tells Lou that he offered to go get some ice cream so that he could have a reason for leaving the house. His wife does not like him doing business during their personal time. Lou says, "You always need a good reason to leave the house, I thought my girl was hard on me." Raymond says, "Women, what are you going to do? Is that you pulling up?" Lou says, "Yes." Raymond chuckles, "You driving a Malibu now?" "It is a friends car ok, that is why I am here, remember? My car is shot the hell up. And why are we still on the phone?"

Lou hangs up the cell phone and gets out of the car. "What`s up Ray? How are you doing?" Raymond replies, "Better than you, I could imagine." "I see you have jokes," Lou replies. Raymond says, "But seriously, it is good to see you." "If I were you, I would be glad to see me too." Raymond snaps back with, "Well, everytime I see you, I do make a little money." Lou says, "Huh, oh now it is only a little money. I think I paid your house off by now. What are we getting you next, a Bentley?"

Raymond replies, "It is a good feeling to be a free man, don`t you think. Lou laughs at him, "You pimping me through the system, I do all of the dirty work. And I pay you to clean it up, right?" Raymond replies, "It sounds like a good partnership to me." They start to Laugh after their little "comedy routine".

"I still can`t make you choke on your words under pressure,"Lou continues. "That is why you pay me the big bucks," Raymond says. Lou replies, "I thought it was little money." "It is, after my wife takes out her cut. She`s the real pimp. And I have to be heading back soon. So start from the top. Tell me everything that happen today. Every detail matters for me to do my job great," Raymond says.

Lou says, "Well, there is not much to go off of... my girl and I were at the superstore shopping. Next thing you know, our phones starts blowing up with calls and texts saying I`ve been killed. We did not believe it at first. When we went outside, we couldn't find my car. Instead of calling the cops, I called my friend Ronnie. He took us home, gave me his daughters car, and a ride back to the crime scene to check it out. Basically, someone is trying to kill me."

"Why didn't you call the police?" Raymond asks.

Lou replies, "I have warrants for my arrest on some traffic bull shit." "Come on Lou," Raymond replies. "I could have handled that for you when it first happened. Let me see what I can do to make that go away. As for the two murders, if what you are saying is true, they should have you on surveillance to clear your name. Now what store were you shopping at again?" Raymond asks. Walmart on Bullard.

I am going to clear your name on the two murders, but the warrants are another issue. With my connections you should be out within three hours once you turn yourself in," Raymond says.

"Man are you sure about this?" Lou asks. He absolutely hates jail, with a passion. Not that anyone loves it, but Lou re-e-a-l-ly hates it. Raymond assures him that he will be back on the streets within a couple of hours tops.

Lou agrees to meet Raymond at his office the following day to arrange to turn himself in to the police. "Excellent, I will drive you there myself," Raymond says. They exchange parting salutations and go their separate ways.

Now it is almost 11 o`clock. Lou's family is safe, and he is going to the police station in the morning. But he is racking his brain trying to figure out who wants him dead. Could it be his past coming back to haunt him.

With all the wrong he has done before turning his life around, there is no telling whom, or what could be the culprit. Bowe told him that the deeper you get into the streets, the harder it is to get out. It does not matter if you have kids, or going to church every day.

Lou knows that he has done to much to change his street perception now. But he has a lot more patience as he has gotten older, and now taking care of his own family.

Lou calls Jason, but gets no answer. Then he calls Trell. Trell is one of the realist guys you will ever meet. Straight forward with you. Right is right and wrong is wrong. A while back, Trell told Lou that Trina looked familar to him, and that she could not be trusted. But he could not recall where he remembered her from, so he dropped the subject.

Trina and Lou fell in love after her parents died in that car crash. Lou was there for her and Corey and the rest is history.

Trell answers on the first ring. "Hello!" Lou says, "What's up?" "You tell me, watching the news shit, they said you were dead, and now you are a subject in a double homicide.

Plus, I called you a few times nigga. So you tell me what's up with you?" "Can I come over?" Lou asks. Trell replies, "Are you alone?" Lou answers, "Yes!" "Come by then." "Ok, I'll be there in fifteen minutes."

Lou starts his drive over to Trell's place, but he uses the time to reflect on all that has been going on around him in the last few weeks. With the hope of drumming up thoughts, that may help him answer some of his questions.

But then, he sees a police patrol car coming up behind him. Lou's heart sinks into his chest. Before, he can respond any further, the police car puts on its flashing lights and siren, moves into the next lane, and speeds pace Lou in response to another call.

Lou's entire body falls into a relaxed sigh of relief.

Chapter 14

Ryder and Money are at "The Truck Stop" getting hammered. They are on their third bucket of Red Stripe and third mixed drink, Crown and Coke.

A bar patron, one of the Regular's, a weathered sixty nine year old dark skinned man, glances at Ryder and says, "You need to mix that Coke with Jack, not Crown. You messing up a good drink. Nobody showed you how to drink yet?"

Ryder replies, "Now I get a lesson on drinking too?" The Regular replies, "I do not know what is wrong with all you young kids. Y'all are messing up everything. With your hair... your cloths, with the pants hanging off your asses, and the music that y'all listen to nowdays, as he tries to rap. "What is it? To the hip and the hop and the hibby?" The Regulars erupt into laughter, "But you went too far when you starting cutting Crown with Coke," he continues.

"Deddie! Deddie, come here sweetheart," as he sweetens his voice for her. Deddie, the bartender, looks his way. "Deddie, give these two kids a Crown, with no

Coke, and put it on my tab will ya?"
Deddie replies, "Ok hun. You boys
want ice?" Before they can answer, a
guy at the bar yells out, "No ice,
straight."

Money feels obligated to buy the
Regular a drink in return. "Now let
me buy you a drink old man. Miss
pretty lady," talking to Deddie.
"Can you make the old man an Adios
Amigo?" "What the hell is that?" The
Regular asks.

Money says, "It is a mixed
drink, something like a Long Island
Iced Tea but blue." "I don`t want
that shit," the Regular says.

Ryder says, "You making us drink
a shot of Crown." The Regular chirps
back, "That's not the same." Money
screams, "What! See, these old
people are stuck in their ways, and
you're ass might be senile." "Who
the fuck are you calling old and
senile?" The Regular yells back.

Ryder just starts laughing at
him. This back and forth went on for
the remainder of the night.

The Regular, Ryder, Money, and
poor Deddie stuck in the middle of
the three of them talking trash.
Ryder needed to take his mind off

his problems. So he entertained the old man all night.

While Lou, finally arrives at Trell's house. He told him what happened, and that he is turning himself in to the police in the morning.

Trell asks him, "So you have no idea who wants you dead? Lou shakes his head no, "It sounds crazy but the cops can help us find out," Trell says. Lou gives him the are you crazy look. Trell continues, "Just think about it, two people are dead. And if you didn't do it, then who? Just let the cops do all of the work until the streets start talking. Whatever comes first. But for now, the police are all we have. You can get lots of answers from them, when they interrogate you. Until then, we can`t make any moves. Don`t worry I have your back...

...It's getting late, so if you need a place to stay for the night, or months, I have a guestroom. Lou replies, "Thanks I will take you up on your offer for tonight. I have a long day tomorrow."

Lou did not get very much sleep that night, knowing that he would be heading to jail, and getting interrogated tomorrow. Even though it was only in the hope of finding who wanted him dead. His only hope was that nothing else popped up when the cops ran his name through the system.

The next morning, Lou meets Raymond at his office. But while Lou spent the night tossing and turning, Raymond called the lead Detective Donald Cobb, to let him know that his client would be turning himself in. Detective Cobb and Lou have some history. The Detective can not believe it.

This is his second chance at getting Lou, and he is not going to miss out this time around.

You see, ten years ago, in the Lower 9th Ward, Lou was in his bedroom asleep... when three armed men broke into his home. They got in through the back door.

Lou normally goes straight to the stash house after scoring Drugs. But this particular night, he had gotten lazy and tired. So he broke one of Uncle Bowe's rules. Never bring the work home.

But Lou was so tired that he went straight home, placed the drugs

he had just purchased on the kitchen
table, took a shower, and went
straight to bed.

Detective Cobb did not know if
Lou was the man, or working for
someone else. So instead of making
the bust as Lou was putting the
Drugs into his car, Detective Cobb
waited to see where Lou was headed.

The cops are getting ready to
kick in his front door, while Lou is
inside sleeping. When... another
cop, spies someone going in through
the back door. So Detective Cobb
orders his team to breach the front
door.

The Cops kick in the front door,
as three guys are breaking into
Lou`s house through the rear door.
One of the robbers grab all the
drugs from the kitchen table, while
the other two look for Lou to kill
him.

The first shot came from outside
of the house, then one of the
robbers shoots a round off in the
house at the cops. The cops start to
fire back.

Yes, there was a shoot out in
Lou`s house between the cops and
three robbers. The robber who took

the drugs from the kitchen table was killed outside of the home with the drug bag in his hands.
The other two got away.

Lou wakes up, dazed confused, shocked, and in a panic, after hearing the gunshots, and being surrounded by cops with guns pointed at him in his own home.

The case against Lou was destroyed since the robbers stealing the drugs saved him from going to jail, and the cops raiding his home ultimately saved his life. Ever since then, Lou changed up a few things, and has been under Detective Cobb's radar.

Chapter 15

When Lou sees Detective Cobb, he knew it was going to be a long day. And indeed it was. Lou gave his statement with his attorney present. Cobb sends two of his detectives to investigate Lou's story, Detective Walker, a very attractive white blond wearing a ponytail, and Jamal Steals, a black cop around six feet tall sporting a 1990's flat top haircut. They come back in two hours. What they saw on the surveillance tape was a shocker. Some more questions needed to be answered.

Thirty minutes after Lou and Trina arrived at the store. A guy in a red Camaro pulls up behind Lou`s car. He gets out of his car, and opens the trunk of Lou`s car.

Places a black bag in the trunk, and grabs a blue and black bag from Lou`s car. The guy gets back into his Camaro and pulls off. This all happens in less than a minute.

Then you see the two boys that were killed walking to Lou`s car. Well the detective knows Lou did not kill the two kids, and Lou`s story checks out. But he has Lou on the ropes right now, and he does not want to let up.

Detective Cobb walks back into the interrogation room, sits across from Lou, and looks him directly into his eyes. "That shit does not work on me. Man can I go now," Lou says. Detective Cobb asks? "What was in that bag?" Lou replies, "What bag? Are you joking right now? What does a bag have to do with a murder investigation? Man! Two people are dead. Clear me so I can go."

Detective Cobb continues, "The bag, has a lot to do with the murder investigation. See, someone put a black bag in the trunk of your car. We have it on tape. When my detectives went to the car pound they found that bag. Guess what was in that bag?

Lou says, "Fuck if I know. I don`t know what type of game you are playing man. And I do not know shit about no bag. I don`t care where you said you found it."

Detective Cobb tries a different approach to try to break Lou. "Well, who is your friend in the red Camaro.

Lou looks over at Raymond. "There they go," he says. Then he looks back over to Detective Cobb, and asks, "What red Camaro? I do not know anything about a red Camaro. I went to buy party supplies from WalMart, that is it."

Detective Cobb, "I knew you were going to say you didn't know what was in the bag. So I will tell you. There were two keys of coke in that bag. Lou says, "Ok, now what does that have to do with me. It is not mine." Detective Cobb, "It has a lot to deal with you. You see your friend just walks to your car opens the trunk. Huh! No key, no remote, can you believe that. Your trunk just pops open right. Who was that guy Louis."

Lou replies, "I don`t know what you are talking about." Detective Cobb says, "Do you need to see the tape to refresh your memory." Raymond finally jumps in and says, "No! No need too. Are you finished? Charge him or free him that is where we are at this point.

Detective Cobb says, "He is free and clear on the two murders for now. But this coke thing, is a new charge that we are dealing with."

Detective Cobb knows that Lou
will not talk or rat on his boys.
But he is having fun with this. He
is now ready to turn up the heat,
but for Lou, playing dumb is
working. All of his answers are, I
do not know what you are talking
bout. Raymond not letting Lou see
the videotape was the best move, and
the Detective knows it.

Detective Cobb asks, "Tell me
something Louis. Maybe it is me. Are
you the victim right now?" Lou
replies, "You tell me." "Ok tell me
this then. Why didn`t you call the
police when you realized your car
was stolen?" Lou says, "I don`t know
I just didn`t?" Detective Cobb
continues with, "Then if you did not
call the police, who did you call?"
Lou says, "A friend." Detective Cobb
asks, "Does that friend have a
name?"

Lou is pissed off now. He is
aggravated and quite. The detective
has Lou right where he wants him.
"You ready to talk?" Asks Detective
Cobb. "Because if I have to run the
license plate to find out your
friend's name, I will," he
continues. "That just takes more
time, but I have all day. Just make
it easier on yourself. Tell me who
is the guy picking you and your

girlfriend up from the store. It is already on tape Louis."

Lou says, "He has nothing to do with this. He just gave us a ride home." Detective Cobb, "That all he did?" Lou replies, "Yes, but why does any of that matter? We had food to put away. So we had to go home first." "So why didn`t you call the police after that?" Detective Cobb presses.

Lou replies, "Because I did not want to go through this bullshit you are putting me through right now. Ok!" "You know you still never reported the car stolen as of now. Why is that?" Ask Detective Cobb. Lou replies, "You'll found it all ready. I am in here, and I don`t want that car anymore. You can have it as a gift."

"Oh, you are talking now, ok, what is your friends name?" Lou replies, "Ronnie." Detective Cobb asks, "Ronnie who? Give me a last name!" "Bell," says Lou. "Like the singer?" The Detective asks. Lou replies, "To be honest, I do not know his last name, or his real name. I never ask him and he never volunteer it."

Detective Cobb calls in one of his detectives to run the license plate on the car Lou got into at the store. Detective Cobb is drilling Lou with all types of questions, but Lou continues to reply that he does not know anything.

Detective Cobb continues to repeat questions like, "Who was that guy in the Camaro? Why didn't you call the police once you got home? Why are you acting like you are hiding something? You _are_ the victim right? How did that guy get into your trunk with a remote or key? Did you leave your trunk open for your friend to drop off the two keys or coke? You never reported the car stolen. So I can not write it up as a stolen car. You gave them your car for all I know. Maybe they just appeared to be breaking into your. Maybe they were running drugs for you, and got killed in a drug deal gone wrong."

Lou says, "Man, you are something else. Are you, really stooping this low to try and dig something up that is not there?" Detective Cobb says, "I am just doing my job Lou, and you can not even answer my simple victim questions. So you must be hiding something."

"I am answering all of your questions, you just refuse to believe me," Lou says. "If I am not saying what you want to hear, then that means I am lying. Right Detective?" Detective Cobb glares at Lou very hard, and then he gets up to walk out of the interrogation room. Lou shares a look with Raymond.

"You told me a couple of hours," Lou says. "Well yes, I did. But you are a free man once they finish interrogating you. You will have to go to court in two months. For the traffic violation and missing your court date. I got the email an hour ago."

Lou asks, "So what do you think they are doing?" "Playing mind games with you," Raymond replies. "Just stick to your same story. Never change your story then you lose all credibility." Lou says, "But it is the truth." "I know it is, but a lie or the truth, never change your story," Raymond adds.

In the past, Raymond has always told Lou to never tell his side off the story, let the police do their job, let them find what they need to take you down, and that they get

paid to investigate. So let them
investigate.

The detective comes back into
the room and says, "Jerome Jock.
You ever heard of that name?"
Lou replies, "No!" Detective Cobb
says, "He is the person that came to
pick you and your girlfriend up. And
you don`t even know him. You called
<u>him</u> before 911, and you do not know
who he is? That don't smell fishy to
you Louis?"

Lou says, "Like I said, we knew
each other on a first name bases. Ok
detective! You did some mighty fine
police work. You now know who picked
my girl and me up from the store.
Now, find out who wants me dead.
Don`t forget detective my car has
tint dark tint. I asked Ronnie to
bring me to the scene and he did. We
drop my girl off at the house first,
and then I called my Lawyer. That is
why I am here now. That is all I
know, and you are still trying to
make me out to be the bad guy in
this."

Detective Cobb says, "This is
not about you, and who wants you
dead. This is bigger than you. Two
kids were found dead in your car,
that you never reported stolen.
Before they steal the car, a guy

with stolen plates pull up, open
your trunk, and put two keys of coke
in it. You see my point of view."

Lou replies, "No I don't, my car
gets shot up from someone thinking
that I am inside, that's what I see.
But hey, I will report the car
stolen if that will make you happy."
Detective Cobb replies, "It is not
going to make me happy, it will just
change the narrative. You are free
to go."

On the way out, Lou sees Ronnie
walking into the police station,
being escorted by two detectives.
The two lock eyes as they walk past
each other. Raymond says, "I told
you they are playing mind games."
Lou says, "I know, but we have been
through a lot. Is Ronnie good?"
Raymond says, "Well I hope so, he
knows what to say."

Our stories will line up. When
it comes to knowing his name or my
name. He does not know me as Louis
Joe Hill. He never asks and I never
volunteer it.

Chapter 16

It is now 4 pm and Trell has been calling Jason since 11 am. He, really needs to talk with him. So he drives over to his home, sees a crime lab van, and yellow tape creating a perimeter outside of the home.

Trell pulls off not knowing what to think, when his cell phone rings. It is Jason number, but it is not Jason on the other end of the call. It is his first cousin Lee who answers. Trell answers the phone speaking as if Jason was on the other end. "Man I have been calling you all day." Lee interrupts him, "This is not Jason." Trell says, "Who is this?"

Lee replies, "This is Lee. I saw you pull up, then pull off. I have Jason`s cell phone I grab it before the cops came." Trell says, "What is going on Lee?" "Jason is dead... someone killed him last night. No forced entry or nothing. They found 4 beers half empty. Three shots to the back of the head."

Trell says, "Can you meet me at the McDonald's around the corner?" Lee says, "Ok, and pulls up to meet Trell 15 minutes later.

Trell sees Lee, he is not
looking too well. Still hurting
after losing his first cousin. Jason
and Lee were very close. Lee knows
everything about Jason. Jason's mom
died when he was four years old.
Lee's mother at the time, was eight
months pregnant with him.

So when Lee was born, Jason has
been there ever since. Lee is a cool
dude. He is chill, stays to himself,
and does not bother anyone. Most of
the time he was too busy cleaning up
Jason's messes. He always had
Jason's back.

Trell knows how close they were,
and now, Trell is hurting also, but
he needs some answers. Right now he
feels that someone is attacking his
old crew. He or Ronnie can be next.
Trell, Ronnie, Jason, Lou, and Mego
called themselves the Get Money
Team. Long before Floyd Mayweather
was the Money Team.

Lou and Jason were still
hustling, but Ronnie and Trell
cashed out. Trell and Lee shook
hands, hugged, and then took a seat.

Trell ordered a sweet tea. Trell
says, "What is going on? How are you
holding up?" Lee replies, "So many

moving parts, but I will work it out." Trell says, "You're telling me. So what all do you know?" Lee says, "Man I came home about 2 am. The door was unlocked, everything looks normal. I walk into the den, and there he was, dead. I took the dope he had left and flush it down the toilet. I grabbed the guns, money, and cell phone. Then I called the police."

Trell asks, "Did he say anything about the people who he had over?" Lee asks, "What do you mean?" Trell says, "Did he tell you that he was having a get-together or something?" "No," Lee says, "But he was excited about a new move... a new connect."

Trell says, "He always getting into some shit. He also said he saw Lou the other night, and he was acting bad or funny with him. He flashed his lights and blew the horn at him. Lou knows that car from any were. Jason had some bitches in the car so he was like fuck it," Lee continues.

Trell asks, "Do you think Lou had something to do with it?" Lee replies, "Or someone else he knows." Trell says, "Lou was at my house last night. You did not hear about

Lou yet?" "No," Lee replies. "What`s up with Lou?" He asks.

Trell tells him about what happened to Lou's car and the story about Lou being dead, and wanted for murder all at the same day.

Lee asks, "Who you'll at war with?" Trell says, "That is what I was calling to talk to him about. Someone is making moves on us. You either coming up---" Lee interrupts, "Or you falling off."

Trell says, "What do you know about that?" Lee says, "Jason always said it. I can hear him now. You either coming up or falling off Lil bro." Trell says, "We are falling off Lee. We are being picked off one by one."

Meanwhile, Detective Cobb is on the phone getting more information on Jerome Jock aka "Ronnie". He hangs up the phone, read over his notes, and walks into the interrogation room. Ronnie looks mad but not worried. Detective Cobb ask Ronnie, "How are you doing? Mr. Jerome Joke I am sorry Jock. Is that right?"

Ronnie peers at him with an evil look. "My name is Detective Cobb.

Can I offer you a soda or bottled water?" Ronnie says, "No I`m good."
The Detective says to Ronnie, "Before I tell you what Lou told me. You wanna tell me your side?"

"My side of what?" Ronnie asks. Detective Cobb, "That is funny. That is the same thing that Lou said. Why do you think you here?" Ronnie replies, "I do not know, you tell me. I`m outside washing my car. Two of your detectives pick me up for questioning. So ask your fucking questions." Ronnie handles the trick question pretty well.

Detective Cobb, "Do you know a Louis Joe Hill?" "No," Ronnie says. "So Louis did not call you yesterday to pick him and his girlfriend up from Walmart ask the detective?" Ronnie says, "You mean Lou? Yeah, I picked Lou up yesterday from Walmart."

"What is Lou's full name, let's start with a simple question?" Ronnie says, "I don`t know." "I have it here. I know his full name. So are you are going to say I don`t know every question? It is a normal startup question. What is your friend Lou's full name?" Detective Cobb asks.

Ronnie says, "I do not know."
Detective Cobb asks, "So Mr. Jock
what do you know? Tell me what
happened once you picked up your
friend Louis?" Ronnie tells the
truth. No need to lie they did
nothing wrong.
Ronnie says, "I took them home.
They had lots of bags. Lou and I
left to check out the story about
his car being shot up an all. We
were at the crime scene for about
fifteen minutes then we left."

Detective Cobb asks, Where did
you'll go next?" Ronnie says,
"Home." "You are free to go," says
the Detective.

He knew he was not going to make
them crack. But it was worth the
shot. Lou's crew is solid. You must
do your job. They will not volunteer
any information. But something is
going on in the streets, and he
knows Lou's crew is in the middle of
it somehow. No proof, all instinct,
and a strong gut feeling. Someone
does want Lou dead but he does not
know who. Finding out who shot those
kids will help Lou. Detective Cobb
realizes that Lou does have a target
on his back.

Chapter 17

Trell is at home when Lou calls. "What is good homie? I am out that bitch! I'm hungry tired. I'm going check on my girl. I will be back over later on tonight."

Trell says, "Ok. It feels good to be a free man right?" Lou replies, "Hell yeah, an hour feels like a year in that place. But I`ll give you a call when I`m heading back your way."

They hang up the phone. Trell didn`t tell Lou about Jason, to confirm Lou did not set Jason up. He feels Lou does not know that Jason is dead. Everyone is a suspect for Jason's death.

Ryder is at home when he gets a call from Tank. Tank is ready to do whatever it takes to keep the coke.

"Any word from Tyson?" Tank ask. Ryder replies, "No." Tank asks, "What about Lou, is he really dead?" "Is he, really dead?" Ryder is irritated by the question, "What do you mean, really dead?" "Bam said that wasn't him in the car."

"What!" Ryder replies. Tank says, "Yeah big bro, it was two

dudes from the east that were in Lou`s car. I think they stole his car. Did Lou kill `em?"

Ryder says, "Slow down! Wait, wait. Lou is still alive?" Tank says, "Yep." Ryder says, "Then he must be laying low. Are you sure?" Ryder ask. Tank replies, "Put the TV on the 5 o`clock news."

Tank walks into the room while still on the phone, and Ryder sees him. "You was here the whole time? I thought you was gone." Tank says, "You have been asleep all day." Ryder says, "I was hungover from last night." Tank says, "It`s on now, look.

Ryder turns the TV volume up. The news reports that two 18-year-old males were gunned down. The owner of the vehicle was released on all charges after turning himself in for questioning.

Ryder texts Lou, after watching the news: "I thought you was dead, call me."

Lou sees the Text. He now knows that everyone knows the real story that he is not dead. Lou does not respond. His mission now is to check on Trina and Corey.

Lou pulls up to the hotel unannounced a little after six o`clock pm. He knocks on the door. "Open the door it`s me." Trina hears that it is Lou on the other side, opens the door, and gives him a big hug and kiss, as if he was gone for ten years.

"Is everything ok, Trina asks. Lou says, "I wish I can truly answer that question, baby I still don`t know anything."

Trina says, "I was so worried about you the whole time. I did not know what to think. I just wanted peace of mind." Lou says, "The police held me for about 5 hours. Asking me all types of questions. Trying to see if the dudes in my car were running drugs for me. I was like, I do not know them."

Trina asks, "Why are they looking into if you sell drugs or not?" "They found two pounds of weed in my car, and the store video camera saw someone opening my trunk, and swapping out bags. The main thing is, how did they open my trunk?" Lou adds.

Trina asks, "Did you leave the trunk open for them to swap out bags?" "Yes," Lou says. "After talking to my uncle. I called my connect, and said yes to more work." "So you deal drugs when you are with me?" She asks. "I was getting more product before I run out. I had a short shipment so I had to do something."

Lou tells Trina a white lie. She knows him for selling weed only. He did not tell her it was two keys of coke. So he changes the subject, "Where is Corey?" "He went for a walk," she says. "Well I just came to check on you'll I am going by Trell's tonight to see what he knows about anything. To see if the streets have been talking, Lou says."

Trina looks at him seductively. "Before you go." She takes off her shirt and starts kissing on Lou. She attacks Lou like a wild animal in heat, takes off his shirt, and pushes him onto the bed.

She unbuckles his pants takes out his penis and starts to give him a blow job. Lou stops her before he gets too excited, flips her, pulls her shorts and panties off, and starts to give her cunnilingus until she has an orgasm. They finish with Lou inserted his penis inside of

her, and fucking her until her legs
start to tremble in orgasm.

Thirty minutes later, and Trina
now asleep. Lou takes a shower, and
leaves to head back to New Orleans.

Byron and Lil Duegie pull up to
Ryder's home. They get out of the
car, walk through the side gate, and
follow marijuana smoke into the back
yard where the find Ryder, Tank,
Money, and Bam.

They greet everyone with
handshakes and hugs. Lil Duegie,
talking to Bam, "You part of the
crew now?" Tank jumps in and says,
"He been part of the crew. That is
my ace." Lil Duegie says, "I have no
problem with him. He works with
Frank, with you? "Ryder is Money's
homie, and Money hooked us up
together," Tank adds. "It's all love
baby," Lil Duegie says.

Tank says, "Oh, ok, I thought
you was trying to start some shit.
With all of that, no new friends
shit. Who came up with that? That is
the dumbest thing I ever heard,"
Ryder sees puzzled looks on a few of
their faces so he breaks down the no
new friend saying to the crew.

"See when you trying to get money. You have to find you a crew. Until you find the right crew. So you need to make new friends. Once you find the team to get money with. When y'all start making lots of money, then, it's no new friends."

Tank says, "Did Lou tell you that too?" Bam chimes in, "But that's real how you broke it down like that."

Tank asks Ryder if Lou called him back. Ryder says, "No, but he good right now. We will hook up." Then Tank brings up Tyson. Ryder says, if he doesn't talk to Lou by tonight they are going to take out Tyson. That same night.

Byron says, "I think someone is starting a war. They are trying to take out your boy Lou. We just finding out the guy we buy our coke from is dead. They killed him in his house."

Bam says, "Ever since them niggas came home from prison. All the big-time dealers have been dropping. They want the streets back." "What are their names?" Byron asks.

Bam says, "I only know of one of the dudes. They all call him War. His brother was killed ten years ago by the cops right before War went to prison. They were robbing your boy Lou. I think he went after Lou, and killed those two dudes in Lou's car.

Ryder says, "So you think he tried to kill Lou. How you know all of this?" "My girl," Bam says. Tank replies, "Your girl!" Bam says, "Yeah nigga, my girl... Ok, follow me. My girl's sister has a friend named, Lora. Lora is cool with Lou's girl Trina. My girl was by their house when the word got out that Lou was murdered. She told me the whole story. It sounds like a movie." Money says, "Small world. So what's going on? What happened?

Bam told the crew what his girl told him. Ryder is shocked, and in a state of confusion. So much on his mind. If Lou does not call him back, he is going to kill Tyson tonight. Which is making him feel worried, since Tyson hasn`t called him all day either.

Maybe Tyson is making his move on him. Who knows what is Tyson`s next move? Now Ryder has more bad news to tell Lou that may change his life.

Ryder does not know if he should tell Lou, but if his life is on the line, he has to tell Lou what he found out. Ryder is still in disbelief. There is no way Bam made up that story. Ryder keeps saying to himself.

Money says to Ryder, "It is time for you to do you. Lou not picking up the phone we either going to do this or not." Lil Duegie says, "I thought you wanted out the game. The way you was talking the other day. Money says, "I just know there is something different, I could be doing. But this is still how I eat." Everyone agrees with Money.

Ryder says, "Tank, Bam... y'all stay here. He looks over to Byron and Lil Duegie and says, "Y'all load up the choppers and meet me at my house in an hour. Money and I are going to ride around Tyson's crib to check out the scene. See who all are out there."

He looks back over to Lil Duegie and Byron and says to them. When you load the guns, make sure to use only the bullets in the boxes, and put some gloves on too.

Chapter 18

Lou pulls up to Trell's house. It is now 9 pm. Trell is taking out the trash. They greet each other and walk inside. Lou takes a seat in the living room. Trell walks in from the kitchen with a six-pack of Red Stripe Beer in his hand, and offers one of them to Lou, before joining him on the couch.

Lou guzzles the entire beer down after his first sip. "Aah, now I am ready to sip on one. Do you have any more?" Lou says. Trell looks at him and says, "Damn, you must have had a rough day." He hands Lou another Red Stripe.

"Man, what happen today?" Trell asks. "Just stressing I guess," Lou replies.

Trell is really trying to read Lou in order to see if he can find out whether or not he killed Jason. So he asks, "When was the last time you spoke with Jason?" Lou replies, "The same night those kids were murdered in my car."

Trell confirms that Lou is not the murderer, based on his reply. Deep down inside, he knew all along that Lou did not do it, but he needed to be sure. So Trell decides that it is a good time to break the news to him.

"Well, my nigga, I passed over there to see what was up with him. I was calling him because I felt like something was wrong. But I did not imaging this." "What are you talking about?" Lou asks. "Jason is dead dude."

The two friends are now heartbroken together, and their eyes are red and want to cry, but they couldn't even if they tried. Death is part of their lifestyle. Kill or be killed. No one is innocent. But it hurts, and somebody must pay for this one. That is their homie for life.

Ronnie, Jason, Trell, and Lou made lots of money together with Mego.

Lou says, "Let me guess, no one knows anything?" Trell replies, "You guessed right. I also spoke to Lee. He called me back from Jason's cellphone. We met up at the McDonald's around the corner from the house. He said that he cleaned up the house before he called the police. If it were anybody else I would have been thinking he was

lying. But he didn`t have to call
me, or let me know anything. You and
I were the last two people to call
Jason."

Lou says, "Jason called me early
yesterday morning. Saying I was
acting funny with him. Then he said,
I will call you back. I have been
waiting on his phone call ever
since."

"What did he want?" Trell asks.
"I don`t know, we barely spoke," Lou
replies." Trell pauses for a moment
to connect the dots, "When I was
talking with Lee today he said Jason
told him that you were acting funny,
and didn't want to stop to holler at
him. He was blowing his horn and
flashing his lights at you."

Lou replies, "That never
happened. I have been getting to bed
on average around 10,11 o`clock
every night. Why would Jason lie?"

"I don`t think Jason lied. He
knew your car, and you know his. So
who was driving your car when you
were sleeping?" Trell asks.

Lou thinks about it for a
moment...

"My girl does not drive, so Corey must have taken my car... Trina's kid brother. He wrecked his car, and Trina told me not to get it fixed right now...

Come to think of it. I could not find my keys that morning, and Corey told me to look in the bathroom. And they were right there where he said they were. I had more gas in my tank than when I left too. Plus my shit was dirty. I just thought I was high, since I smoke a lot of weed...

So the question is, what does an eighteen-year-old kid sneaking my car out, have to do with Jason's death, and those kids getting killed in my car?"

Trell says, "Probably nothing, but call him up and ask him, where they were that night and in what part of town?"

Lou calls Corey's cellphone. Corey picks up. "Hello!" Lou says, "What's going on?" "Nothing. Laying down watching TV," Corey replies.

Lou sees Corey more as a little brother, so it is normally hard for him to talk about anything besides video games and sports with him, so even though this involves more dire

circumstances, Lou still takes a
measured approach.

"Look, Corey, I am not mad or
anything... I know you took my car
the other night. But I need you to
answer a question for me? Did a guy
pull up behind you, or did you see
anyone flashing their lights or
blowing their horn at you?"

"Wow!!!" Corey's mind is blown
just by the fact that Lou knows
this, so he immediately spills the
beans on his little caper a few
nights back. "Yes. I was coming from
a house party across the river."
"What happened that night?" Lou
asks. "On the way home, some car
came out of the blue blowing and
flashing the lights. Then, the car
made a right on General de Gaulle
Boulevard."

"Thank you for being honest with
me. Where is your sister? She is
knocked out, do you want me to wake
her up for you?" "Nah, that's ok, I
will talk to y'all later."

Lou tells Trell everything that
he and Corey spoke about. Trell
takes a moment to think about what
is going on without saying anything.

Lou breaks the silence with, "You have a cigar? I need to roll up something for my head." Trell says, "Yes I do," and offers Lou one of two cigars his holding in his hands.

Lou rolls some weed and they smoke the night away, until they pass out.

Lou forgets to call Ryder back, so Ryder says fuck it. Now, he is making his move on Tyson before Tyson moves on him.

Ryder and Money are in the car rolling through Tyson's hood. The car creeps so slowly that they appear to be almost floating. They park two blocks away from Tyson's home, because no one is outside.

Money asks Ryder, "Are you ready to call it a night since no one is outside?" Ryder looks at Money, and then he calls Lil Duegie to ask him what he sees.

The clock on the car's dashboard reads that it is 2 am. Lil Duegie and Byron are ready for the moment, locked, loaded, and ready to shoot. He tells them, "Once you make the block shoot it up."

Then Ryder turns his attention back to Money and tells him, "Get ready." Money replies, "For what?" "The fireworks," Ryder adds.

Byron drives down a one way street, Lil Duegie gets out of the car, makes a left turn and stops the car in front of the house, and Lil Duegie starts to shoot up the right side of the house. Byron fires through the front door and the windows.

Someone opens fire on Byron's car, and Lil Duegie aims at that person to start shooting at them while running back to the car to make a rapid departure from the scene. Ryder sees what is happening, and tells Money to hop into the back seat.

Lil Duegie and Byron are driving away, as several guys are running out of the house with guns in tote.

They start loading themselves into a large car to chase Lil Deugie and Byron, but Money and Ryder pull up beside them before they can take off.

They open fire on the entire car, and as Ryder drives off, Money continues to fire on the car and the house again, before driving away.

The next morning, Lou and Trell are now smoking whatever they did not smoke the night before, when Trell's phone begins to ring. It is Ronnie. "You sleep?" Trell says, "Just getting up dog. Lou and I are blowing on some gas."

Ronnie says, "I am on my way." Trell says, "Hello? Hello? Ronnie had already hung up the phone. Ronnie sounded pissed. I think he knows about Jason.
Lou replies, "Then he must have been only a block away, because he is pulling up right now," Lou says, while looking out of the front window.

Ronnie walks into the house pissed off. "They kill Jason man." Trell says. "When?" Ronnie asks.

Trell replies, "I don`t know. I just found out yesterday." "What is going on? Are we next?" Ronnie asks.

Trell says, "What is going on? Man we do not know anything right now, so calm your ass down, and hit this weed, because three heads are better than two."

The three friends smoke their weed without much talking.

Now three hours later. Trell asks Lou, "What time did Jason call you the morning that Corey had your car?"

Lou thinks for a moment and says, "I guess about 9:30. Why you ask?" Trell replies, "Check your call log." Lou looks down at his phone and sees that it was at 9:41 a.m., so he tells Trell.

Trell tells Lou to call Lee, but Lee does not answer the phone. This provokes Ronnie to say, "Alright, you are going to have tell us what you are thinking."

Trell looks at Lou and says, "You said that Jason was waiting on a phone call... I want to know who he was waiting for. I just hope Lee did not delete Jason's call log. If he called you at 9:41. Then they called him at 9:43 to 9:45."

They are intrigued by Trell's detective work. So, Lou inquisitively says, "Right. The power of the tree does it again," he continues.

Lee calls back ten minutes later. Lee answers, "Who is this?!!" It's me... Trell, why you have to answer the phone so angry all the time." "Oh, what's up? My bad, I didn't know it was you. I have to lock in your number."

Trell says, "You do that, but I have to ask you something. Do you still have Jason's cell phone?" Lee replies, "Yeah, it`s right here." "Well go back a day. Look for a phone call to Lou at 9:41 am. Then, give me the number of the person who call him after that... 9:43 or something in that time frame."

Lee says, "Ok I have the number, it is (504)655-XXXX. Trell says, "Got it. Thanks" Lee asks, "You think that is the number of the killers?" "I do not, but it is a start?" Trell responds.

They hang up the phone.

Trell asks himself, "Where do they have a payphone? Let's call the number from a payphone." Lou asks, "Then what Trell, see if they answer?" Ronnie says, "It is only a number. What can we do with a number?" "I don't know, maybe it can lead us to something... look, are we

going to call the number or what?"
Trell asks.

"Ok, fuck it, let's go find a
payphone," Lou blurts out. Ronnie
says, "Y'all go find a payphone. I
have to go home. I have not been
home since I was picked up by the
those asshole cops. They told me I
was not under arrest so I could
follow them to the station."

"What happen with that?" Lou
asks. Ronnie replies, "We good, I
told them everything they already
knew." Lou says, "I will be dropping
off the car later. I am getting a
rental car today." "Ok y'all be
safe, I am going home."

Ronnie walks out of the door,
and Trell and Lou gather their
things to head out to pick up the
rental car.

On the way to Canal street.
Trell sees a payphone. He asks Lou
to pull over so he can call the
number, and Lou does just that.

Trell gets out and walks over to
the payphone, while Lou waits in the
car.

Trell calls the number, but no
one answers. So he waits for a

moment to see if they will call back. He turns towards the car to see Lou giving him the hurry up look.

It is obvious that Lou thinks this is a waste of time, and he is willing to go along with Trell's whim because of Jason. But calling a number from Jason's phone, when Jason sold Coke, makes him a bit unsettled.

Trell is the kind of guy that moves to his own beat, and is very instinctive. So Lou knows better than to underestimate him. Trell gets into the car.

Lou says, "What happen?" "No answer," Trell replies.

It looks like another dead end. They pull off and go straight to the car rental. Lou asks Trell to follow him to drive Ronnie`s daughter's car back to Ronnie`s house.

Trell and Lou pulls up to Ronnie`s house, and Ronnie`s daughter, Kelly, is outside. Lou gets out of the car, and asks Kelly where can he find her dad? And Kelly replies, "He went to the store for my mom." Trell says, "Here are your car keys."

Kelly replies, "I can't drive it anyway, I am still on punishment." Trell says, "So do you want me to keep the car." Kelly quickly says, "No! I will be off punishment this week." Lou laughs at her, "Ok then. Tell your dad we will see him later." Trell gets into Lou's rental car, and they drive away.

Lou asks Trell what is next. "Just take me home for now." Lou says, "Alright. I guess I will do the same. Go lay low. Go by my girl and relax a little."

On the way to Trell`s house.

Lou can not help but notice a car following them. Trell is sleeping. Out like a light, just that fast. Although, he <u>is</u> as high as the sky.

Lou utters, "Trell, man get up!" Trell says, "I`m not sleep I was meditating. "You always... meditating," Lou responds. "That's what I do," Trell says.

Lou says, "M-a-a-a-n I think we are being followed." Trell looks over his shoulder and says, "By who?" Lou says, "I don`t know."

Trell looks at him and says, "Man are you alright?" Lou continues to look through his rearview mirror, and says, "Yes!" Trell adds, "Then don`t go to my house. Jump on the interstate, and head west on I/10."

Lou says, "I hope you have a plan." "I think I do." Lou asks, "Where are we going? Trell replies, "To Ohio." "I know you are not talking about the state, so what is Ohio?" Trell says, "You will see."

Lou asks, "See what?" "If they make it to Ohio, then we know that we are being followed." "What are you up to?" Lou continues.

"Making sure we are not being followed," Trell says.

Trell pulls out his phone to make a call. He is calling Coope. One of Trell's hitters, aka "Hit Man".

He asks Coope if he can meet him at Ohio. Coope says, "We are already here. Chilling and hanging out." Trell replies, "Where is Deno?" "Right here." Trell says, "Good, y'all get ready." He hangs up the phone.

Lou knows Trell is up to something. So he just does what Trell says to do in this situation.

Trell looks at Lou and says to him, "Get off on Williams Boulevard. Then make a right on Vets. A left by the dollar store. A right on Airport. Go to the end of the block, turn right, and take me home. Nobody will be following us. That is for sure. If you chase a wolf it will lead you to the pack."

Lou says, "You think we went to far?" Trell says, "No! They already took it this far. Jason is dead, and you were a target already... car shot up and all. That really could have been you. We do not know anything. We are so far removed from the streets, we don't even know the word on the streets. Remember when we knew who was going to get killed soon by the way they were moving? We knew what was going to happen before it happened. So I feel like we are being attacked by someone. So we will watch the news to see who it was."

It is now 2 pm on a blistering hot and humid Monday afternoon. Tank is at Bam's house and they are talking about last night. Tank is mad that Ryder did not let him go on the caper. Bam does not believe anything happened.

They have not seen or spoken to Ryder since they split up last night. Tank suggests that they go drive by Tyson's hood, and see who is on the block.

Bam replies, "That is quite possibly the dumbest idea ever. You are going to get us killed." "How?" Tank asks. "Those dudes are on red alert. If your brother hit them up last night."

Tank, "I guess you're right." Bam suggests that they go chill over at his girlfriend's house.

"Sometimes she has her friends over there hanging out. I would fuck 'em all, if they let me," Bam says. Tank is not as sexually charged as Bam, so he does not respond to Bam's assertions.

"One thing that is for sure, the odds are in your favor to meet somebody," he continues. Tank replies, "Hell yeah."

They arrive at Bam's girlfriend house twenty minutes later. As they drive up to the house Trina is walking out to her car. Tank and Bam do not know that is Trina. They just see a fine looking woman leaving the house. They wait in the car for Trina`s parking spot.

When she is out of view, they get out of the car, and walk into the house. Lora tells her that Bam is outside. Lora is Terry's older sister Sabrina's friend. Sabrina is older than Terry by seven years. Terry goes outside to meet them.

This is Terry and Lora's first time meeting Tank. They share introductions and go inside to sit in the living room area. Lora asks Tank, "How old you are?" And Tank says, "I am sixteen, why do you ask?" "You came over here to see which one of Terry's friends you can get with huh?"

Tank was not shy like a lot of teenage boys, when they spoke to females that were many years older than them. But since he was always raised to be respectful to women, speaking to her was natural and not persuasive.

"I am just hanging with my homeboy that's all. But who was that leaving out of the house? She is hot," Tanks says. Lora looks at him as if to say, "child please".

And then she says, "Boy please, she is too old for you. What she given you can't handle," Lora says. Tank looks at her as if he is taking control of her with his eyes, before he says, "She will have to tell me that personally... I like older women," as he continues to lure Lora in with he stare."

Lora breaks out of his spell before saying, "Don`t be looking at me like that." Tank replies, "Like what?"

Bam starts to laugh, but Terry jumps into the conversation before this gets out of hand. "That is my sister's best friend Trina..." and then she looks directly at Tank," ...and she got a man." Tank says, "Ok, I understand."

Bam utters, "That is Lou's girl." Tank says, "Man, Lou has good taste in women." Lora asks, "So you know Lou or something?" Tank, "Not really, but my older brother does." Lora says, "Well, I just told her, that her ex-boyfriend's older brother, is the one who shot up Lou's car." Lora tells the rest of the story about Trina and Lou until...

Terry's older sister, Sabrina, walks through the door and says, "Where is Trina?" Terry replies, "You just missed her." Sabrina walks back out the door.

Bam says, "Ah, so what did she say when you told her about her ex?" "She thinks Lou is going to leave her if she tells him." Tank says, "Or kill her." Lora screams, "What! You think Lou would do something like that?"

Tank humbly replies, "I do not know, but she is foul for what she did."

Tank was right about the entire premise of Lou's relationship.

"It was all based on a lie that targeted Lou as a mark in a robbery caper," Tank says. "Damn. That is messed up," he continues. Imagine, having your car shot up... then, at the same time, going through this emotional conundrum that puts the love of your life, at the center of a plot that nearly has you murdered."

Lora looks at Tank in disbelief, shakes her head, and says, "How old are you again. You spend a lot of time around older people, don't you?" "Yep, I used to spend a lot of time with my grandparents when I was a kid. During the summer I could stay up to watch episodes of Murder She Wrote..." Then, Tank pauses in a moment of realization. "I guess that is why I like older women," He says.

Terry looks at him and once again comes in to regulate, "Stop flirting with Lora," she says." "Stop hating," Bam says to her. "It is time for you to take your friend home," she replies.

Lora and Tank are still talking about Lou and Trina's issues, and were not even paying attention to the conversation between Terry and Bam.

"Well, I hope they make it through this situation," Lora says.

Tank replies, "Well, from what I heard, the cops saved Lou`s life, because when they got there... one of the three dudes there to rob Lou, got away with the dope. The cops shot him outside, which basically meant it was no longer Lou's dope. The other dudes were getting ready to kill Lou, when the cops kicked in the door to raid the place."

Tank is starting to get more into the story now.

Everybody says they were going to kill him, and that is mentally hard to overcome, although that story has been told many times in the hood.

But the Police kicking in your front door, at the same time you are being robbed, and about to be murdered?

Tank and Bam continue to hang out with Lora and Terry, while Ryder and Money are eating dinner at a restaurant not too far from a hotel they rented last night.

They got rid of the two stolen cars from last night, and have already checked out of the hotel. Now they are waiting on Byron and Lil Duegie to come and pick them up.

Ryder receives a phone call from Toya, Tyson's baby sister and Frank's cousin but he does not answer. Money asks the waiter to turn up the volume on the television.

The 5 O`clock news is on, and the Anchorman reports the breaking news, "Two off duty rookie NOPD officer's were gunned down in Kenner while sitting inside of their vehicle. The ambush took place in broad day light."

Neighbors say that it is a safe neighborhood, and nothing like that ever happens there. One of them stated that, "It sounded like World War II," as one retired veteran said, as he described the gunshots that he heard.

Ryder says to Money, "Toya just call my phone." Money says, "What do you think she wants?"

Ryder replies, "Well, since we just shot up her brother's house, plus Frank getting killed the other day. She probably is going through it. I will call her back later tonight though."

Money asks, "She don`t know anything right?" Ryder says, "Boyyy I hope not. My heart did jump when I saw her number."

Money says, "Make sure you get all the info you can out of her when you call her back. I did not see Tyson out there last night." "Me either," Ryder replies.

Money says, "You think we got him in the house?" Ryder is thinking. "Well whenever you call Toya back, we will know what is going on," Money continues.

Lou is at Trell's house, and they are also watching the news.

Trell looks over to Lou, and says, "That is who was following us." Lou replies, "We messed up this time?" "Calm down, all we did was pick up a rental car. Went for a ride and came home. That is all we did today."

Lou says, "Alright then, why would off duty cops be following us? Someone with some money is attacking us." "So whomever it is behind all of this, knows we must have taken them out," Trell adds.

Lou says, "They were paid to follow us. You think it is our old friends in the police department. Trying to take us out? I mean I do not know, but why would they? We left the game on good terms.

Trell replies, "Bo, man, I believe he work for the Feds now."

"Really!" Lou says. "Do you think he will flip? Nah, not on

us... after all we did for him, and all of the money we made together?"

Trell replies, "Right now Lou, everyone is my enemy outside of you and Ronnie. If a person has the potential to hurt us. That is how I am going to treat the situation. Because, we do not know what is going on. Understand this much Lou, besides Jason, no one was hustling anymore. So we should not be a treat to dudes on the streets selling dope."

Lou replies, "You are right. So what do we do now?" Trell ponders... "Well, the way I see it, we keep a low profile and locked and loaded ready to shoot.

Chapter 19

Detective Cobb is on the phone with the Kenner police department. He is trying to get in contact with the lead detective, because he wants to know first hand what happened to the two off duty police officers. Unfortunately, he is having a hard time getting an answer.

When he finally gets through, he discovers that no one knows who is working the case as of yet. So he decides to drive to the Kenner P.D. to speak to someone in person.

When Cobb arrives, Jenkins, an officer that went through the police academy with him, recognizes Cobb when he gets out his car. They talk for about five minutes before Cobb asks Jenkins about the two off duty cops.

Jenkins tells Cobb that the lead detective on that case is Detective Janet Hall. Cobb wants to know how he can get in touch with her, so Jenkins gives Cobb her cell phone number, and asks him to follow him to his desk, as the two old buddies head into the station.

After spending some time catching up with his friend Jenkins,

Detective Cobb calls the lead detective, a woman of color by the name of, Janet Hall, as soon as he gets back to his car. She answers on the first ring. "Detective Janet Hall, how can I help you?"

Cobb replies, "Yes, this is detective Donald Cobb with the New Orleans Police Department. Detective Hall says, "How can I help you Detective?" "Well, I am calling about the two off duty officers that were killed yesterday, and I was told you were the lead detective on the case," Cobb says.

"That is correct. Do you have some information for me," Detective Hall says. Cobb says, "NO! But we are working on cases that may overlap." "What do you mean"" She asks. "Some of the circumstances in my case, may be related to your case," he continues.

Cobb goes on to explain about the two kids that were killed the same way a few days ago. He suggests that something is going on in New Orleans, and that there has been a lot of murders since the two kids were killed.

"Last night three guys were killed in their car the same way.

Their house was shot up really bad, and three more bodies were found inside of the house. If possible, I would like to take a look at your crime scene photos once there are ready," he suggests.

Detective Hall says, "Sure, no problem. Can you meet me at the department?" "I am already here, outside." Detective Hall says, "Ok then, give me about ten minutes." They hang up the phone, and an hour later Detective Hall shows up.

When she walks into the station Detective Cobb is talking with Jenkins while he waits for her. Jenkins introduces the two detectives to each other. Then, Detective Hall leads Detective Cobb to her office. Detective Cobb is taken back by Detective Hall's beauty, so he is initially uncomfortable during their walk to her office.

Even though he thinks she is pretty and sexy as hell, Cobb is a by the book kind of guy, so he plays it cool and stays professional.

Detective Hall says, "Sorry it took me so long. I know I told you ten minutes." Cobb replies, "That is ok, it was worth the wait." He is

really speaking to the eye candy
that she presents. Detective Hall
asks, "What is worth the wait?" Cobb
is quick to clean up his Freudian
slip. "The case... getting possible
info on the case is worth the wait.
We must solve this."

Janet says, "I know. I am so
sick of people being quiet. It is
very difficult to get people to talk
about this." "What about cellphone
records," asks Cobb. "Waiting on
that now. I am tracing all calls
from the last three days."

Cobb replies, "That should lead
to something. The most frequent
calls will get you a little closer.
I just know our cases are related, I
have a gut feeling."

Everything is telling Detective
Cobb, that Lou and his crew are
behind all of these shootings.

He believes that Lou, Trell,
Ronnie, and Jason have been ghosts
until now. None of them have been in
any major trouble until now. But,
Lou's car being shot up, and Jason
being murdered... they are being
attacked. So did they strike back
and kill the three guys in the car,
and shot up their house.

Detective Cobb has no clue about any of his thoughts. He is just guessing right now.

Once in Detective Hall's office, Detective Cobb takes a look at the pictures, but nothing comes of it. He gives Detective Hall his card and tells her to call him if she hear's anything.

The next day, Detective Hall call Detective Cobb. And what she tells him makes his hairs stand up. Detective Hall informs him that the cellphone records show that the last number received on one of the officers' cell phones traces back to a payphone at a store on Rampart street.

Detective Hall is at the store viewing the store's surveillance tape. The tape shows a guy wearing a New Orleans Saints hat and sunglasses. It also shows the license plate of the vehicle, so Detective Hall calls in to run the license plate. The information shows that the car is registered to Jerome Jock.

She calls Detective Cobb to share the news. "I can not believe this. We just had him in custody. Their friend was just murdered, and now this." "I need to see that tape, Detective Cobb says." "Ok, but I am not at the department so I will come to you. Give me about an hour," she says.

Detective Cobb is eager to see the footage, and Janet shows up two hours later. The only thing on Detective Cobb's mind is the tape that Janet has. She walks into Detective Cobb`s office.

Detective Hall says, "Hey you! Sorry it took me so long. Had to pick my kid up from school. Then bring her to my sister's house." Cobb replies, "That is ok. Things happen in life we have no control over. How many kids do you have?" He asks. "Only one. She is nine years old," she says.

Detective Cobb takes the opportunity to share with her that he has two boys that are twelve and seventeen. Detective Hall says, "You have young men." Cobb starts to laugh, "They are a hand full, I know that."

Detective Cobb notices Detective Hall carrying more than a videotape in her hands. "What is all of that?" She replies, I hear you are a good detective, so I have more photos from the crime scene. But, I didn't see anything. So here you go. Now everything I know, you have."

"Thank you, Detective Hall. Let's cue up that video first," he says.

They watch the tapes. Detective Cobb sees everything that Detective Hall said was on the tape. He tell her that is not Jerome Jock on the payphone. "So who do you think it is?" She asks. Cobb replies, "I can not tell with the hat and glasses on, so we move on Jerome Jock. He must be the driver."

Detectives Hall and Cobb drive to Jerome Jock's house. When they pull up to the house they see the same Chevy Malibu from the videotape. Kelly, Ronnie`s daughter is outside on the phone. She is not very street smart person, and has been sheltered from the real world, so she does not know about her dad's past lifestyle.

The two detectives walk up to Kelly flashing their badges, and ask to speak with her father. Kelly says, "He is not home." "Do you know when he will be back?" Asks Detective Hall. Kelly replies, "No he just left without saying anything."

Detective Cobb points over to the Chevy Malibu and asks, "Who does that car belong to?" Kelly responds with, "Oh! That is my car." Detective Cobb says, "Really, where did you go the last time you drove your car?" "I think the Mall. I don`t remember. I haven`t driven it in almost a month." "Why not?" Detective Hall ask. "I am on punishment."

Detective Cobb asks, "So who has been driving your car?" Kelly replies, "My dad`s friend, they brought it back yesterday." Cobb asks, "Who was driving your car?" She says, "Trell and...

Before she can say, Lou, Ronnie's wife, Tina comes outside and interrupts Kelly before she can finish.

"What the hell is going on out here?" Detective Cobb, "Hey, how are you doing we are looking for your husband. Do you know his where about's?" She replies, "No I do not, and I do not appreciate you questioning my daughter like this, without my permission. She is a minor."

Cobb realizes he has rubbed her the wrong way, says, "I apologize ma'me. Can you tell your husband to come down to the station for a few more questions when he gets back?" "I will let him know," she says.

The two detective leave, and Tina turns her attention to Kelly, and asks, "What did they ask you, and what did you say?" Kelly tells her mom everything she told the detectives. "Go inside Kelly," she says.

Tina calls Ronnie right away, and Ronnie answers the phone. Tina says, "What the hell is going on that the police keep coming by the house?" Ronnie says, "Hold on baby. What do you mean?" Tina says, "The police, they came by. They just left." "What did they want?" He asks,

Tina says, "Negro, you. Again! If you are guilty of something, do not come home. The police may be watching the house," she says. Ronnie replies, "I am good I did not do anything." "What about your friends? Because they were asking about Kelly`s car. She told them that Trell dropped it off at the house... and you told me that you gave it to Lou. Right?" She says.

Ronnie replies, "Damn, you sound like the cops. Trell and Lou were together when they dropped the car off. Lou is in a rental car now." "Then I guess they will be looking for Trell now," she adds.

"Trell! Why... what did Trell do?" Tina says, "I do not know, you tell me. Just be lucky I came outside when I did. Your daughter would have answered every question they asked." Ronnie says, "Thanks, babe. Let me call you back. I need to call Trell and Lou."

Ronnie calls Lou's phone while driving to Trell`s house. Lou does not answer his phone and Trell is not home. Ronnie calls Trell's phone and he does not answer. But Ronnie does not leave his house.

He is confused and left to ponder what is going on. Ronnie is a changed man. He got out the game and put away lots of cash from when he was in the streets hustling.

When he met his wife, after about a year of going out, the relationship became very serious. Ronnie started giving Tina all of the money he was making, and he only had enough money on him to get more drugs.

Tina started t invest the money in abandon houses and paying independent contractors cash to renovate them. She would buy them using her name and credit. She also rebuilt Ronnie's credit, at a time when Ronnie was not even thinking about credit.

Tina bought six properties while Ronnie was in the streets. Before Ronnie knew it, his girlfriend was bringing in ten thousand dollars a month renting out the six houses. All of them were duplexes. She would deposit the rent money into her bank account, and pay the mortgages with money orders from the money Ronnie gave her.

She did this for five years using street hustler contractors that she knew would not be filing taxes. When Ronnie saw how much money she had in the bank, he asked her to marry him. Tina said no. She did not want to marry a drug dealer. So he decided to get out of the game.

Trell calls Ronnie back within ten minutes. Ronnie answers the phone pissed off. "Man! What the hell is going on? The cops came by my house twice already looking for me. This time asking about my daughter's car. What did y'all do in my daughters car?"

Trell says, "All we did was, stop at the rental car place, a payphone, and from there your house." Ronnie says, "Are you sure?" Trell answers, "Yes dude. You tripping right now."

Ronnie replies, "Well, I think I have the right to be tripping. I don`t know what is going on. Also, I think the police may be looking for you right now. So don`t be tripping."

"Me! Why me?" Trell asks Ronnie. "They caught Kelly outside by herself, and asked her about the car. She said you dropped the car off at the house. That is all she told them before Tina came outside and saved the day. Where are you?"

Trell says, "At the boxing gym. I am on my way. Where is Lou?" "He is going to check on his girl." "Ronnie says, "Don`t leave! I will see you when I get there," and they hang up the phone.

Now, Trell is thinking about what could have lead the cops to

Ronnie's house. Did Lou do something
he did not know about? Does someone
really wants Lou dead, or is he just
 covering it up? Did Lou kill those
dudes in the car? Man! Ronnie got me
 tripping, Trell thinks to himself,
while punching on a heavy beg. Lou's
           good... I think.

      Ronnie is driving and also
thinking to himself. Trying to help
 motherfucker's now I am in a jam.
Jason is dead, Lou's car is shot up,
   and he is missing in action. Who
   would want him dead anyway? Well,
 you don't know people like we think
we do these days. Ronnie is pulling
up to the boxing gym. He calls Lou's
        phone again. No answer.

Chapter 20

Lou is at the hotel in Biloxi Mississippi, sleeping and laying low with no idea what is going on with Trell and Ronnie. He forgot his phone in the car. Trina is laying next to him. She has the answer to all of his problems. She knows who shot up his car, but does not know how to tell him because it goes deeper than that. She does not know how he would react.

Corey is watching television, as they are all sharing the same hotel room. He is bored out of his mind, so he asks Trina if he can go to Popeye`s to get some chicken. Trina says yes, and asks Lou for the car keys. Lou is tired and in a daze, so she grabs the car keys and hands them to Corey.

Trell calls Lou`s phone as Corey gets into the Car. Corey presses ignore on the phone. He also sees 10 missed calls on Lou`s cellphone. He turns the ringer off, and leaves without giving Lou his cell phone. He feels that Lou will have to leave right away, and take the car. Corey, being selfish in the moment, leaves and goes to Popeye`s.

Now at the gym, Ronnie calls Lou`s cellphone again, while Corey is in Popeye`s eating. Lou's cellphone is still in the Car. Ronnie says to himself, "He pressed ignore on me... maybe he is on the phone."

Ronnie walks into the gym to find Trell still working out. "I see you in here trying to stay positive... well I`m not. You think someone wants him dead." Trell says, "Well, he did get his car shot up, and that usually means someone wants you dead." Ronnie replies, "True, but he could have set it up himself."

Trell says, "Ok, even if I wanted to believe that, why would he?" "I don`t know, maybe we know too much. So we could be next." Trell says, "You are not making any sense." "I can`t even go home right now, and the cops may be looking for you now, so now what?"

Trell says, "If all your daughter said was Trell, they can not link my nickname to my real name." Ronnie replies "You obviously do not watch the "First 48" they do it all the time." "Yeah, but that is only for murder cases. We did not kill anybody," Trell says, even though he is thinking to himself that even a broken clock is right twice a day.

So he concedes to Ronnie, "I guess you are right... so I can not go home either. Just to be safe."

Back in Biloxi, Corey is leaving Popeye`s, and heads to the beach to see what is going on, on a Tuesday. When he gets there, he sees college students hanging out, so he parks the car and gets out to take a stroll on the beach.

He sees plenty of hot chicks in bikini`s. Corey feels as though he hit the jackpot. A frisbee hits him in the head.

Before he can make out what happened, he hears a voice say to him, "I am so sorry. Are you ok?" Corey looks up and sees the hottest girl in the world looking at him. He is at a loss for words. He wanted to say yes. But he just kept staring at her. "Are you ok?" Corey says, "I don`t know. I mean, yes, yes I`m ok... wow, you are so pretty. I just had to let you know that."

The Girl asks, "Where are you from? I have never seen you before." "I am from New Orleans." She replies, "I thought so. I can tell by the accent. My name is Alondra." She extends her hand for a handshake, and Corey says, "I am Corey." The two of them hit it off, and they begin to have a great conversation.

He discovers that Alonda is starting her freshmen year at Mississippi State University, and she wants to be a nurse. When she asks Corey what were his plans, he lies and says that he attends LSU. He has a feeling that playing video games would not impress her.

But at that moment he realizes that Trina was right all along. A girl that he was interested in would make Corey look at his life more seriously in the span of one conversation. Corey tells her that he has to bring the car back to the hotel. He asks for Alonda's number. She gives it to him, and Corey hurries back to the Hotel. He has been gone for two hours now.

While Corey is on the way back, Ronnie calls Lou`s cellphone again. Ronnie and Trell are still at the boxing gym. Ronnie says, "I think we must be bothering him. He just pressed ignore on me. I know when someone presses ignore on me. My wife does it all the time when she gets mad at me. It's a half a ring." Trell says, "Maybe he is getting some pussy... or what if he is in trouble?" Trell's phone rings. "Is that, that bitch ass nigga?" Ronnie asks. "No, it`s Lee."

Lee is calling to let Trell know about Jason`s funeral. It is Saturday at ten o`clock a.m. Lee only knows a few people outside the family, so he asks Trell to let his real friends know the real-time and date. The newspaper will have the time wrong and date on purpose, so he tells them to not read the newspaper.

Ronnie is still mad as hell at Lou. He not answering the phone. Now Ronnie has Trell second-guessing Lou`s loyalty. "What did Lee want?" Ronnie asks. Trell replies, "To tell us about Jason's funeral." Ronnie says with a heavy heart, "I can not believe Jason is gone. Man our crew is getting picked off. The cops are looking for us. I do not know how much trouble we are in... Man, what did you'll do in my car?"

Trell starts to get irritated by Ronnie excessively asking the same question. "I told you already. You are tripping." Ronnie says, "Well it links back to me."

Trell replies, "What links back to you?" Ronnie says, "Nothing! Did you say you all did not do anything in my car?" "Yes, and that is the truth." Ronnie replies, "Well nothing should lead back to me."
Trell looks at him, and says, "I am starting to think something is wrong with you dude." Ronnie says, "My dad always said, people will call you crazy before they admit you telling the truth. Where the hell is Lou? He is off somewhere safe and shit. You might be working with him for all I know."

Trell says, "Really dude! I am working with him. Then so are you. You picked him up from the store." Ronnie says, "We did no crime. I could have been his Uber driver. Do not blame this on me." Trell says, "I am not blaming you. Our friend was in a jam, and we both did a small part to this point. When you help a person that is still in the game. You are now part of the game again. I am out of the game too. Lou had no one else to call."

Where is he? That is what I want to know. Call that nigga again and

see if he will be there for us."
Trell says, "Whatever man."

Corey walks back into the room,
and finds Lou now in the room alone.
"Where is Trina?" He asks Corey. "I
don`t know, she was here when I
left."

Then he gives Lou the cellphone.
Lou sees all of the missed calls
from Ronnie and Trell.

He call them back right away on
Trell's phone to explain that he
left his cell phone in the car.
Ronnie is in the background talking
trash. Ronnie says, "It is your
fault we are in this mess. The
police are not looking for you. You
with your girl. All safe and shit.

Lou says, "Tell that bitch ass
nigga to shut the hell up. I will be
back in the city by eight o`clock.

Chapter 20

Meanwhile back in Kenner,
Louisiana. Detective Hall is
tracking down Trell. She is trying
to get information on his real name.
So she needs Jerome Jock aka Ronnie
to identify Trell. At the same time,
Detective Cobb is back at his office
in New Orleans looking over
Detective Hall`s case. Mainly the
crime scene photos of the two off
duty cops.

After hours of looking at
photos, Detective Cobb falls asleep
at his desk with the photos in his
hand, while sitting upright. A knock
on his door causes him to jump up
out of his sleep. He knocks all of
the photos onto the floor.

"Come in!" Detective Cobb says.
It is Detective Walker, still
wearing her blonde ponytail, and
looking sexier than usual. She
stopped by to bring him a cup of
coffee, since he has not left his
office in a while.

Detective Walker notices him on
his knees picking up photos, so she
gives him a hand picking up the
pictures from the floor. She notices
the license plate from the red

Camaro, and tells the detective that she came to check on him.

She says, "I see you are trying hard to find out who killed those kids." Detective Cobb gets up off of the floor and says, "These are photos of Barry Vault and Jose Hernandez, the off duty officers that were murdered in Kenner," he says.

Detective Walker asks, "Are you sure you did not make a mistake, and mix the two crime scene photos up? Detective Cobb says, "Yes I am sure. I am helping out the lead detective on the case in Kenner. She gave me everything you see here."

Detective Walker says, "Well if you are sure, that she gave you the photos of the license plate of the two off duty cops, that is the same license plate number that was on the red Camaro."

Detective Cobb's ears perk up, "Really, are you sure." Cobb can not believe what he is hearing. He rushes over to his file cabinet, gets the case files of the two dead kids. He compares the two photos and sees the same license plate number LYK538 on both photos.

Detective Cobb always had a feeling that the two cases were linked together somehow, but now he has proof. The same license plate on the Camaro that was on the videotape from the parking lot where Lou's car was stolen. Is on the car of the two dead officers.

But the person on the videotape from the parking lot was heavy set, the two cops are slim built, and they were also rookies. So, were they dirty cops? Did they work for Lou on the low? Do they have more dirty cops in this department? Detective Cobb has so many more questions than answers.

Detective Cobb instructs Detective Walker to keep quite about their discovery. He begins to think that his department is dirty. He chooses to keep his focus on Lou at the moment, and keep the license plate connection silent until he can get more information. He does not want to tip anyone off. Now the hunt is on for Lou. No evidence for an arrest, he just needs to ask Lou some more questions.

Detective Cobb calls Detective Hall to tell her everything that he knows. She asks Detective Cobb to tell her all that he knows about Louis. "Can you prove that he is connected. If he already denied knowing the person who put the cocaine in his car, and how are you going to get him to talk?" She asks. Detective Cobb says, "You are right. He must admit that the cocaine was for him, and we both know that will never happen. Besides he has one of the best lawyers in the city."

Detective Hall suggests that they hand their cases over to the F.B.I. "If you do not get him to talk, then we have nothing. But maybe we can pick them all up on a Rico. Then offer immunity for their testimonies, against all of the dirty cops. They will walk away free and clean."

Detective Cobb says, "The Feds will have to agree on that deal. But before we get them involved, let me hunt down Louis and Jerome. One of them can tell us Trell's real name.

Chapter 21

Trina is going through an emotional roller coaster. She does love Lou, but when he finds out the truth about how they met. That she also helped set him up to be robbed and killed... that the dude that got killed that night was her boyfriend, and the ones that got away were her boyfriend`s big brother, War, and his best friend. Who knows how Lou will react to this.

Trina knows that she must tell Lou the truth, since that information can save his life. She can still lose him to death or prison, because when Lou finds out, he will go find and kill War. But when it`s all said and done. Will Lou leave her.

Trina does not want to lose Lou, and she feels that all of the trust that he has in her will be gone. She knows that it is hard to gain Lou`s trust after he been burned.

Even if he stays, she knows the relationship will be dead. He will be a different man. So she will tell him when she makes it back to the room.

Trina had to get away for some fresh air while Lou was sleep. She took a walk around the hotel and walked to a nearby Chinese restaurant. When she returns to the room with the food, Lou is gone. She asks Corey, "Where is Lou?" "He said he is going back to New Orleans," Corey replies.

Trina does not want to tell him this information on a phone call, this is something that she needs to do face to face. So she texts Lou that they need to talk when he returns. Lou looks at the text but does not reply.

He is parking the car, as Ronnie and Trell are talking. Ronnie is pissed off still. He says to Trell, "There go that bitch ass nigga." Trell laughs and says to Ronnie, "Let it go. Let's just see what is going on."

It is a warm and humid Tuesday night with no wind blowing at all. Lou gets out the car and says, "Why are you'll outside. It is hot as hell out here." Ronnie says to Lou, "We are the ones asking the questions. How you going to come around here barking orders. You said you will be here at about eight o`clock it almost nine O`clock."

Lou says, "If you have a curfew, well get your ass home then." Trell thinks to himself, why did he say that to Ronnie. Lou does not know what is going on.

Ronnie could not get his words out fast enough. So many thoughts came to his mouth at one time that he choked up. He says to Lou very soft and slow, "I can`t go home." Lou says, "Trell, what is this fool talking about."

Ronnie cuts Trell off, "Nothing! You'll do nothing, right Lou?" Trell says, "He thinks that we did something in his car." Lou says, "We did not do anything in your car. We left Trell's house, went to pick up my rental car, and drove to your house. That is all." Ronnie says, "Trell said you'll stop at a payphone." Lou says, "Really Ronnie! We did on the way to the rental place.

Trell tells Lou that the police visited Ronnie's house looking for him. Ronnie says, "Yeah, and my daughter was outside. She said they asked about her car. But because you'll "did nothing" in my car, I can`t go home. Now they may be looking for Trell." Trell says to

Lou, "Kelly told them I dropped the car off right before Tina came outside. So they may be looking for me also." Ronnie says aloud, "But you know who they are not looking for?"

Right now, Lou is lost for words. It is no longer about him. He does not know what to say or do. All he knows is that he has their backs.

Lou, Trell, and Ronnie are good friends. Now the cops may be looking for them. Lou says to the guys, "Can we go inside now, it is hot as hell tonight." Lou's phone rings while the three friends walk inside of the boxing gym. It is Ryder.

Lou answers the phone. Finally. While Ryder is receiving a text from Tank that read: "I have some news for you. Can you pick me up from Bam's girlfriends house? Uptown, 1027 Louisiana Street."

Lou says, "Hello... Hello!" Ryder says, "My bad, I was reading a text from my little bro'. I am going uptown to pick him up."

Lou says, "Well be careful in that part of the city. I do not trust nothing uptown." Ryder replies, "I feel that. That is why I

am going to pick his ass up right
now. But man, when I grab Lil bro'
we need to meet up." Lou says, "Meet
me on the Lake, I will leave where I
am at in fifteen minutes. That
should give you enough time to pick
up Tank.

Ronnie says out loud, "We are
going to the lake now?" Lou looks at
him and says, "No I am going to the
lake." Ronnie says, "No, we are
going to the lake with you. Where
you go, we go my buddy."

Trell starts laughing because
Ronnie is serious, and the face he
is making when talking to Lou is
priceless. Ronnie wants to go home.
So he needs to know what is going
on.

Right now, Ronnie is letting
Trell know what is about to happen
while looking at Lou. "Since he
disappeared for a year." Ronnie is
exaggerated and actually means for a
day. But before he can finish, Lou
says, "Come on, I don`t have
anything to hide."

Ronnie says, "If you are doing
reverse psychology it is not working
we coming." Lou says, "Come on
then."

Lou is walking back into the boxing gym. Ronnie ask Lou, "Where are you going, the car is this way?" Lou reply, "If you want to wait in the car here are the keys." "I thought we were on our way to the lake," Ronnie replies.

"We are leaving in fifteen minutes like I said in the conversation when you were eavesdropping. Is that ok with you?" Lou says. "Well, to me it seems like you were about to leave right away, before we volunteered to ride alone. Now all of a sudden..."

Trell jumps in to shut this back and forth shit down, "Y'all both need to shut the hell up. Ronnie I have been hearing you cry all day." Ronnie says to Trell, "Cry, me cry, he brainwashed you. You forgot what he did to us motherfucker."

Lou replies, "What the hell did I do to us? Trell what the hell is he talking about?"

"How can you forget this fast? We can not go home." "So it is my fault, Lou says. "Hell yeah it is your fault," Ronnie replies.

"Like I said, until I know what is going on me and Trell are going everywhere you go. And don`t be asking for gas money."

Ronnie continues to talk trash as they get into the car to meet with Ryder.

Trina is at the hotel, getting ready for bed. Corey is in the shower. She is still worried about her conversation with Lou, so she decides to give Tina a call. Tina answers the phone, while she is in bed watching television.

"Hello." Trina says, "Hey girl, I hope I didn`t wake you up. Tina, "No I am just watching TV. What`s up, tell me what is going on." Trina says, "Is it that obvious that something is going on." Tina replies, "Yes, you sound scared. Talk to me. I feel it in the air also. Ronnie is out for the night. He just gave me a call. Lou and Trell are with him.

Trina says, "I think once I tell Lou what is going on, he will leave me." Trina breaks down into tears.

Tina says, "Well, tell me what`s going on." Trina says, "You know the story... about the night the cops kick down the door to Lou's house". Tina says, "You talking about when

the police save your lives that
night when one person was killed and
the other guys got away?

Trina says, "Yes. That night.
Well..." Trina pauses for a long
time as she starts to cry even
harder. Tina is being patient as she
tries to comfort and encourage her
to take her time. Tina says, "Girl
just let it out." Trina tries to
pull herself together to gather her
thoughts. Trina says, "The guy that
got killed that night was my
boyfriend at the time." Tina
replies, "What do you mean your
boyfriend? Trina continues, "I
helped set up the robbery."

Tina is at a loss for words. She
does not know what to make of the
situation. "I know what I did was
wrong, but I was much younger, and
now, I have to save his life by
telling him the truth. Because I do
love him." Tina says, "And how is
telling him the truth going to save
his life."
Trina takes another pause before
saying, "Well, the guy that shot up
Lou`s car was my ex-boyfriend's
older brother, War." "How do you
know that?" Tina asks. My best
friend Lora is dating one of his
friends. They met at my ex-
boyfriend`s repast.

Tina says, "I just talk to my husband. He told me he has no idea what is going on, and you have all the answers to their situation. So why are the police asking about my daughter`s car?" Trina replies, "I do not know anything about that. Only who shoot up Lou`s car."

"Well you need to tell them before you get my husband killed, or I will," Tina says. Trina replies, "See, now you even hate me. Tina says, "I don`t hate you, I just don`t know you anymore. I thought you were a square."

Trina says, "I had no one else to lean on after I lost my parents in that car accident. Lou was all I had. The girl Lou knows was me acting." Tina replies, "So let me get this straight. All these years you have been pretending to be sweet and innocent?" "Yes, at first... I want a clean slate. He is the love of my life now," Trina says.

Tina asks, "If he were broke, would you still want him?" Trina pause.

Tina says to Trina, "Just like everybody else, you are in love with the lifestyle." Trina responds, "And the dick." "Look who is being honest for once," Tina says.

Tina says, "If I were in your situation. When you tell him the truth. You must tell him right away. So when you do speak with him, start by showing him the real you. He fell in love with a fraud person. Let him feel the way he feels once you tell him what is going on. Don`t worry about him leaving you. He has a lot on his mind right now...

...you did what I said to do already. You have rental property plus money put away. You are good as far as living on your own is concerned. But, you need to just... start being yourself again. If not for Lou, then do it for yourself. It must be miserable living a lie, because that sweetheart shit, is over."

Tina starts to get a call on the other line. "Ronnie is calling me now, I will call you back." "Are you going to tell him?" Trina asks.

Tina says, "Yes, but I will make him promise not to tell Lou, you have to do that." Trina asks, "Why are you going to tell him?" Tina replies, "Because he is my husband, I love him, and he needs to know

now... so at least someone will know what is going on. I will call you back."

Corey is getting out of the shower as Trina hangs up with Tina. Trina says, "We are leaving in the morning to go back home. "I will be glad all of this is over," Corey says.

Trina thinks to herself, it is just getting started.

"What time is Lou coming back to pick us up?" Corey asks. Trina replies, "I am renting another car in the morning." Corey asks, "When did you start driving again?" "I had to go back to New Orleans the other day to pick up something from my friend Lora," she says. Corey looks at Trina and says, "You seem different. What is up with you?" Trina says, "My stomach hurts that's all.

CHAPTER 22

It is Tuesday 10:30 pm, Ryder and Tank are on the way to meet with Lou. Tank told Ryder what he learn for Lora. Ryder could not believe what he was hearing. Ryder just does not want to tell Lou, because he is not sure himself. So Ryder asks Tank to tell Lou what he just told him, and Tank agrees to relay the story to Lou. Meanwhile, Ronnie is relaying the same story to Trell via Tina. Trell says to Ronnie, "I had a bad gut feeling about her. She was too good to be true."

Ronnie promises his wife not to tell Lou, so he told Trell instead. Ronnie also made Trell promise not to tell Lou right away. Trell feels bad about not telling Lou, but if Trina does not tell Lou by tomorrow afternoon, he intends to come clean and tell him everything.

Lou is on the phone with his uncle Bowe, and tells him that his crew needs a place to sleep for the night. Bowe tells him they can stay at his place for the night, and that he will leave the key under the doormat.

Lou hangs up the phone just as Ryder and Tank are pulling up. Trell and Ronnie are skipping rocks into the lake like big kids. The balmy night is made more miserable by the biting mosquitos. Now everyone knows what is going on except for Lou.

Ryder and Tank get out of the car, and walk towards Lou, while Trell and Ronnie continue to throw rocks into the lake.

Ronnie notice Trell meeting with Ryder and Tank. He looks at Trell, and says, "Come on. I want to hear what they are talking about."

Ronnie starts to walk toward Lou, and Trell is right behind him. Lou introduces Trell and Ronnie to Ryder and Tank. They have never really met, they just know of each other.

Lou is explaining why he did not answer his phone to Ryder. Everyone else is just listening. Ryder explains to Lou that he made a move on someone. Lou asks, "What do you mean by that?" Ryder says, "I did not know what to do, so I shot up the nigga's house and car.

Trell asked Ryder, "What happened and what was the dude's name? Ryder told them everything that has happened since Lou's car was shot up. Trell says, "Ryder you did the right thing."

Lou says, "A lot of blood was spilled in these two days. Well, I have some business for you and your crew. I was wondering how I was going to move all of this coke, but as you were talking, you solved my problem. We just lost a close friend. His name was Jason." Ryder says, "I am sorry for your loss."

Tank says, "I think I met him before. If he sold coke it is the same person ToTo got his work from." Lou says, "He did his thing. But I will give you the details later this week, on our start date. Just do you with what you have for now. It is getting late, so we will be getting out of here."

Tank says, "Wait, there is more."

Ronnie says, "Like what?" Ryder says to Lou, "Do you know Lora?" Lou replies, "Yeah, that is my girl's best friend. Why what did she do? Tank replies, "Nothing. It is what she told me when I was over there. I was there all day today. When I first got there your girl was leaving out of the house."

Lou is confused. "Who left out of the house, your girl? My girl was leaving from Sabrina's house today? That is impossible. She does not drive." Tank says to Lou, "I waited until she left so I can get her parking spot. I did not know that was your girl until Lora told me."

Lou asks Tank, "So what were you doing over there?" "I was hanging out with my boy Bam, his girlfriend is Sabrina's younger sister. Lora was telling us that War is the person who shot up your car.

Trell says, "I heard of him. But why would he want to shoot Lou?" Tank is tired of beating around the bush so he just comes out and says what everyone else knows. "Lou, your girl set you up that night the cops kick in the door." Lou replies, "Know fuckin' way. That is bullshit. My girl would never turn state on me. I would have been locked up."

Tank says, "No the robbery part. The dude that got killed that night was her boyfriend at the time, and War's younger brother."

Lou is having a hard time digesting this info and does not want to believe it. Then Ronnie says, "I just found out tonight. My wife called me and told me everything. Trina confessed to her about everything. She is going to tell you about it tomorrow."

Trell says to Lou, "Ronnie just told me when we were over there throwing rocks. I was going to tell you tomorrow if she did not tell you. I know you not thinking straight, and probably messed up in the head right now, so I will drive us tonight."

Lou says, "I am good. I just need some rest. Come on let's go." Ryder says, "Are you sure you ok man?" Lou says, "I`m good."

Lou does not want to believe what is going on, and he wants to call Trina, but he is willing to wait until she comes clean.

Lou, Trell, and Ronnie get into the car drive over to Bowe's place, as Ryder and Tank drive away in the opposite direction.

The next morning Trina rents a car. She and Corey pack up, and head back to New Orleans. Meanwhile, Lou is lying down in the bed thinking about what he just learned about Trina. Ronnie and Trell are downstairs talking to Uncle Bowe.

They like to hear about Bowe's gangster stories. Like the one when he got shot in the head, and his crew kidnapped a doctor to save him. Bowe says Lou normally be up by now. You'll must have had a long day yesterday. Ronnie says we had a crazy few days. Trell says I will go check on him, to see if he is still breathing.

Bowe says, "No need for all of that I am sure he is fine. Let him rest." Ronnie says, "Well, if you know what we know. Checking on him is not a bad idea." Bowe replies, "I don`t."

Trell says, "We should let Lou tell you." Bowe says, "If its juice, tell me now. He tells me everything anyway." Ronnie looks at Trell, and moves his head forward as if to say go ahead and tell him. "Trell says, "Ok this is what we know as of now...""

While Trell is giving Bowe the information about what is going on, Lou's phone rings. It is Trina.

She does not know that Lou knows what happened or who she is. Lou answers the phone as if nothing happen.

"Hey what's up?" She replies, "Nothing just checking on you." Trina knows in her heart she is about to lose Lou. So she is appreciating this vibe. This is something she will miss it.

Lou asks, "Are you in a car right now? Trina says, "Yes. I am going back to the house." " Why?" He replies. "Because we need to talk. You may hate me for what I did." "So, it`s true," Lou says.

"Is what true?" Trina asks. Lou replies, "You might as well just tell me now."

Trina starts to cry, because she knows that proverbial jig is up. "Please do not make me tell you over the phone," she begs. Lou says, "Ok, you got that. I have a busy day today, so we can hook up about 6 o`clock." Trina says, "Ok. Talk to you later."

They hang up the phone without saying I LOVE YOU. For the first time since they first started telling each other I love you.

A snapshot of them after they hang up the phone reveals that they both are feeling melancholy about the situation. Lou just realizing all of the rumors are true, and Trina realizing she just lost Lou.

Corey sees his big sister drying her eyes. So he asks if she is ok, but Trina tries to reassure him that she is fine, but Corey knows differently.

"Do you want me to drive, you are not looking so good?" Without saying a word Trina pulls the car over to the side of the road. Gets out of driver's seat and switched places so that Corey can drive the rest of the way.

Trina says to Corey, "We may be moving out of the house for good. But we all we have in this world. That is why I need you to get an education, so you can help me, in a man's world."

Corey asks her, "What are you talking about sis'? You are starting to scare me." "Corey, Lou is about to leave me. Well, he already left me, I think he knows, I just haven't confirmed it yet." "Confirmed what?" Corey asks. Trina begins to jog his memory, "Do you remember my first boyfriend?" "Yes, Bobby, the cops killed him right?" Corey replies. "Yes," Trina says.

"Well, I was there that night. I was not at home like I told you. I was with Lou that night. At his house. So you were cheating on Bobby with Lou. No, Corey, I was part of the robbery. I help set Lou up and how lucky can one person be. The police had a search warrant the night of the robbery and killed Bobby when he was leaving out of the house with drugs that he stole from Lou. But his brother got away."

Corey is a little confused, because all he knows is that her childhood boyfriend was killed by the police. But he lets Trina continue to speak as if he is fully following the story. Eventually, he can piece it all together.

She explains that the police let her go, and she was home before he was awake. Corey says, "So Bobby and his brother robbed Lou, and you posed as his girlfriend?"

Trina replies, "Yes! All I did was unlock the back door, and make sure he was naked with no gun nearby. I just acted like everything scared me and made me nervous so he could protect me. That is one of the ways a woman knows that a man cares for her. He will care about anything that makes you uncomfortable. But women these days call men like that ducks, stupid, or simps. When they are showcasing their loyalty."

Trina looks over at Corey with a set of motherly eyes, and says, "Corey, always treat women well. Listen to her, but never follow her. That is how I know Lou was strong, and the one for me. He listened to me, but he is not afraid to make the final decisions."

Trina is speaking as if this may be the last time she gets to have a heart to heart conversation with Corey, so she puts her best thoughts into the conversation.

She explains to Corey how Lou always had things set up in a way, that if she were to ever leave him, I would have to start all over.

Trina says, "The house we live in, is in his mother's name. Everything is in his mothers name. Corey says, "This whole time you were scamming." Shaking his head in disbelief.

The way Corey put it, it made Trina think about how she was, and who she had become. But she says to Corey, "I did what I had to do. We lost our parents right after, remember that. He was getting money at the time, and he was feeling me.

Corey cut her off and finishes her sentence, "So you stayed with him for the money. Trina says, "Yes, for us. But the way you put it, Corey, you are making me realize the way he is looking at it. I am a fake that posed as the woman he loves, and I am not her anymore." Corey says, "That is a good thing right? Now it is time to be real."

"How do you think he is going to take it?" Trina asks Corey. Corey is shocked, "You are asking me for advice? Who are you?" Trina smiles at him, "Ok, you got me I`m just scared." Corey has never seen his sister like this ever. So he tells her, "You are the best big sister ever in my eyes. I understand you did what you did for us. Lou is good to us and always has. He will be crushed. It is crazy how the people that do the most for you get hurt the worst by you."

There is brief reflective silence between the two of them when Corey asks, "Sis', how do you feel about Lou after all these years?" "He is the love of my life," she says. "I now know it will be hard for me to fill his shoes."

Meanwhile, Lou finally gets up and goes downstairs. He sees Trell rolling up some weed, Ronnie eating an egg sandwich, and Bowe feeding the dog. Bowe yells, "Finally got up huh?" Lou replies, "I was up just thinking." "And how'd that work out for you. It should be a law only certain people are allowed to do an activity like that. Thinking is serious business, Bowe says.

Lou has no choice but to laugh at Bowe's assessment. "Very funny," he says. Ronnie says. "Want an egg sandwich?" No, I am good," Lou says.

Trell looks over at Lou with a rolled blunt in his hand and says, "I got what you want right here." Lou says, "Light it up."

They all go to the smoking section of the house. Bowe has a fresh Dominican cigar to toke, while Lou and his crew smoke that fat blunt Trell rolled up.

Bowe looks at Lou and asks, "Did you speak with Al yet? It is Wednesday. Lou says, "I was going through so much at the time. I did not answer the phone when he called."

Trell says, "Al jammed you up to move coke for him." Lou replies, "Al said to me in so many words. He know we robbed him back when we were getting started. But since we kept re-upping with him, he let it play out. And right before that, he tells me that Mego is dead.

Ronnie says, "Damn, did Al have Mego killed." "He said he died on his motorbike," Lou says. Trell asks, "Do you believe him?" "I do not know what to believe right now."

Bowe asks,"What is your next move? Are you planning on staying with her?" Lou looks surprised that Bowe knows about his Trina problem.

Ronnie says, "Trell told him everything." Lou looks at the two of them and shakes his head. Lou looks at Trell, and says, "What would you do in this situation?"

Trell asks, "Lou, do you really want to know? I would kill her. It would hurt, but fuck her. The police are the reason you still alive and that nigga is dead.

Ronnie says, "Damn man, kill her? Really?" "You damned right." You never liked her anyway, Ronnie says to Trell. "So of course you will say that."

Trell adds, "Don`t forget she never liked me first." Ronnie looks at Lou and says, "Talking to my wife, she says Trina did what she had to do. For her and Corey to survive. She loves you, and that she was young at the time, and Trina says, you taught her so much.

"Sounds like a fucking Hallmark card to me," Trell says. Bowe jumps in to lend and older wiser voice of reason. "Look Neph', just listen to your heart. I feel where Trell is coming from, although not with the same degree of hate," as he looks in Trell's direction shaking his head.

"Ta Ta was in my driveway one morning when I woke up. A puppy that someone left abandon. My grandkids begged me to keep him. As I was trying to find him a home, I invested time with him. Feeding him, walking him, teaching him to potty outside and not inside, etc. After spending all of that time with him...

...one day my grandkids asked to keep Ta Ta at their house. I said hell no, that is my dog. Tell your parents to buy you a dog, and you train it. I love that dog. You see guys, time is the ex-factor."

Lou knows in his heart that he has spent too much time with Trina to give up on her now. Everything is perfect, and it can stay that way if only he can find the strength to forgive her for the attempted murder.

Lou sits quietly not saying anything. Trell says, "Call me weak. But, people are always sorry once they get caught." Ronnie says to Trell, "You never had a dog, huh?"

Everyone starts to laugh, and Lou needed a good laugh after the week he has had so far. He understands that his love life is different than the streets. So he must still handle his business.

Now Lou has more pieces to his street puzzle. He knows, but not for sure, that War and whoever he was with, tried to kill him. But why? Lou decides to call Ryder to find out where Sabrina lives.

Lou plans to watch her house, and see who is coming and going. His thinking is that Lora is very attractive and not from the streets, so whoever she is dating, could be the person feeding her information. That is the only way she will know something like that.

Trell says, "We are getting closer to the truth. Action must be next. We need to strap up. It is time to hunt." Ronnie looks at Trell and says, "You always wanna shoot people. The police are looking for us. So we do not need to be riding with guns."

Trell says, "So what do you wanna do once we find out the truth. Because, if we are not going to do shit, then let's stop looking for who did it." Lou says, "Oh, we are going to do something about."

Lou explains to everyone about the deal he made with Al G Heat, and that all he needed to do is set it up.

Chapter 23

Tyson was in jail the night of the shooting. He was arrested for a DWI. When he got out of jail he was shocked, to find out that six members of his crew were shot, with three dead, and the others fighting for their lives in the hospital. The reality is that Tyson has done so much dirt on the streets to get where he is, that in his mind anyone could have done it.

Frank's killers are the number one suspect. But even still, he needs a crew. His crew is down and out. Tyson, for the first time, is feeling like he is the next target. Now that he is out of jail he just needs to lay low for a while. His crew was gunned down, but he knows that they wanted him.

Tyson goes to his mother's house to relax for a while. Toya is in the kitchen cooking breakfast. Ever since Frank was murdered she has been staying at her mothers house as well.

Everything in Tyson's home was seized after Ryder and his crew's drive-up massacre. They took his cars, money, and guns. Tyson is looking through his call history to see if something gives him a clue.

He sees missed calls from ToTo. He gives ToTo a call. ToTo is at his family's bar cleaning up after a busy Tuesday night. His younger brother Joe is with him. Joe is restocking when ToTo's phone rings. ToTo answers the Phone once he see Tyson's number.

"What`s up homie." Tyson says, "I saw that I missed your calls." ToTo replies, "Yes, I call to check on you once I heard what happen." "I was fucked up by the news myself. I was in jail the night of the shooting. What is the word on the streets."

ToTo changes his voice a little as he spills the street gossip. "To be real, no one is talking. Them niggas the family is beefin' with, were in Vegas, and they still are. I wish I can say they did it... they may have killed Frank, but they did not hit your spot.

Tyson says, "I need a gun and some weed." ToTo says, "Come by the bar tomorrow, I have a 9mm you can have. It`s clean too," Tyson says, "Not for long." ToTo says, "Yeah

nigga, I know what that means. I`m
glad you alright. Plus I know what
you going through... the whole team
shot up. Just hang in there for now,
and lay low, people think you're
dead anyway."

"I guess you right. But who?
What about War, the dude that just
came out?" Tyson asks. "Who the fuck
is that?" Tyson replies, I don`t
know the nigga either. I heard a
jailhouse rumor. Some nigga named
War is taking back over the streets.

ToTo says, "Let me call you
back I have a delivery." Tyson, "Ok,
get at me tomorrow."

While the delivery driver,
Joe, is unloading the cases of beer,
ToTo asks him if he knows a guy
named War and that he thought he
just came home from prison, and Joe
replies, "That name has been ringing
around the hood lately. Why what's
up?" "I just got off of the phone
with Tyson. They just shot his house
up. He is coming to pick up a gun. I
need you to give it to him for me."
Joe asks, "Tyson thinks War made a
move on him?" ToTo replies, "I don`t
think so."

Meanwhile, Ryder and Tank are in the car driving to pick up Tank's car.

Tank tells Ryder, "I have a guy that is going to fix the car in front of the house later on today. So why all of the rushing? It is my car anyway... I can handle my own business... I am a man. And a host of other things to show I am a man..."

Ryder says, "Shut the hell up. I don`t know what is going on, but Lou just asked me for Lora's address. I forwarded him the address you texted me last night. I do not want you, or your car around that house for right now."

Tank says, "It is going down like that? Look, ask that nigga Lou what is up because my homie is chilling with his girl over there. He is over there a lot."

"I am pretty sure he does not want to hurt anyone who lives in that house. It is something to do with his girl. If I have to take a guess," Ryder says. Tank says, "I guess you are right."

Lil Duegie calls Ryder as they approach Tank's car. He needs some more coke.

Since the death of Frank and Jason, plus Tyson not moving anymore, the streets are looking for the coke. They need the rest of the coke that Ryder has. Byron is screaming in the background, "We can`t keep it in our hands." Bam is also texting Tank. He also needs more coke.

Ryder asks if they need it now? They simultaneously say, "Right Now." Business is indeed booming for the moment. Ryder says, I am not at home right now.

Lil Duegie says, "Well, can you go home, we will meet you there in twenty minutes. You are about to make thirty thousand right now." Ryder says, "Well shit, since you put it like that. Ok, I am on my way to the spot now."

Ryder looks at Tank and says, "I am going to drop you off at your car. Wait for the tow truck to come." Tank says, "What is so important that now you have to leave me in my car, after all of that... big bad Lou is coming stuff?" Ryder replies, thirty thousand. Tank says,

"You sold the whole brick?" "Yeah, Why?"

"Bam just called he is out too," Tank says. "We have about sixteen ounces left, right?" Ryder asks. "Wrong," Tank says. We have a nine-ounce plus the brick," he adds.

Ryder asks, Where is Bam now?" Tank says, "Inside of the house." "Tell him to come outside." Tank says, "I did already, there he is now."

Bam gets into the car. "You boys move fast." Tank says, "We were outside when you were texting."

Tank asks Bam if he thought Terry could give the car keys to the tow truck driver for him, so they can go back to the house, and get the rest of the work for him.

Bam looks at Tank and says, "Give me your keys, she will do it." Tank says, "Let her know you are going to call her when the driver shows up. The driver has my brother's number."

Bam says, "Should I write all of that down." Ryder laughs at Bam`s comment.

Bam rushes up the porch and to the front door to give Terry the car keys and instructions. Then he jumps off of the porch on his way back to the car. The car pulls off. A short while later they meet up with Lil Duegie and Byron at Ryder`s house.

Ryder pulls up as he can see Lil Duegie and Byron already waiting outside on the front porch. They chill on the steps for a few minutes. Byron asks, "Where is Money?" Ryder says to Byron, "I think he is going to look at a building for our night club. I gave him all the control. I just wanna see the money return back fast."

Lil Duegie says, "If you'll get that night club going we'll help you'll get the name get out there. All I have to do is serve nigga, at you'll spot for a little while until it gets well known."

Ryder says, "I would say that is a dumb idea. But I can see that maybe working. It would work." Now he sees the full vision, "Plus strong drinks at a good price, a smoke section for V.I.P`s, fuck it the whole club is V.I.P`s. We can have a smoke out night." Tank says, "I thought, you were going legal? Ryder says, "Shut up, you always say

something to mess it up. Come on,
let go inside and handle the
business."

They enter the house and follow
Ryder down the hallway to the back.
Tank grabs the duffle bag, takes out
the whole brick of coke, and gives
it to Byron. Lil Duegie asks to see
it, then goes into his pocket to
take out an unfolded stack of cash.

"How much is that Tank?" Lil
Duegie asks. "Say twenty thousand,"
he adds. Tank says, "Well it is
thirty. Byron says, "We know nigga,
I have the rest." Byron goes into
his pocket and pulls out the other
ten grand. Tank says, "Good, because
we are not going to start that
coming up short shit today. That is
why we still homies. You'll do good
business."
Lil Duegie says to Tank, "If I
ask Ryder to front it to me I bet he
would." Ryder starts laughing. Tank
says, "Now why would he do that,
when you just paid him?"

Lil Duegie says, "Not now if I
take a loss or something happens."
Tank says, "Of course you good for
it." Byron asks Ryder, "What is left
in the bag?"

Tank gives the rest of the coke to Bam. Bam says, "For me, I get to keep all of this?" Tank says, "Make sure you bring back eight grand. Bam says, "Ok I am on. What is the weight?" Tank says, "Nine ounces.

Ryder looks at everyone and says, "Lou is about to be on with the coke. I am waiting on a start date. We just told him about his girl too. He took it well, but it could be that he was in shock."

Tank says, "She did him bad." The crew chat for a little while longer before leaving the house.

Chapter 24

Al G Heat is in Dallas, Texas at his home. He is speaking with his nephew, Juker. They have a plane to catch at 3 o`clock. Juker is packing a few things that they may need for the trip to New Orleans. Al is going to meet the guy who will be moving his coke. Juker met him in prison.

Juker has finally convinced his Uncle to let him take over his cocaine business in New Orleans. The same coke Lou and his crew are waiting on.

Al saw that Lou was being investigated by detectives, and had his face slathered all over the news, so he deemed Lou to hot to deal with at the moment.

This is the window that was needed when Al decided to let Juker run New Orleans. Al says to Juker," I am going to stay home. No need for me to go down there. Just let me know your moves before you move on anyone. That is all I ask. Also, find out what happened with Barry and Jose. I paid them good money in advance. I want to know who did it." Juker has a crazed look on his face when he mentions Barry and Jose.

Juker does not have the heart to let Al know that he had Barry and Jose follow Lou.

Juker had slipped Al's cellphone away when they were in New Orleans. Al had called Lou after seeing the news, but Lou did not answer.

Juker had seen his uncle type in his password a million times, so once Al dozed off for a nap, Juker texted Barry to follow Lou. He also told Barry to delete the text. Juker deleted the conversation from Al's phone. Juker had also given the order for them to find out about Jason.

But they were killed before they could find out what happened the night of Jason's murder. Jason was going to be working with them on moving the coke, but at the time, his uncle Al was still trying to convince Lou to move the product for him.

Juker does not know that Lou and Jason are friends. Lou was going to give all of the coke to Jason, since that was his business lane.

Al asks Juker for the name of the person he will be working with, in New Orleans, and he tells him

that his name is War. Al says to
Juker, "Is that his real name.

Juker replies, "He never asked
for my driver's license, and I never
asked for his. Are you sure you do
not want to meet him today?" Juker
asks Al.

Al says, "Nah, this is your
operation now." Juker asks Al if he
can have his new driver give him a
ride to the airport. Al agrees and
takes the drive to the airport with
Juker.
Meanwhile, War is at his
warehouse meeting with his crew, but
in a party-like setting. He is
letting everyone know that he has a
big shipment coming in, and that he
has two guys he needs them to meet.

This is the reason for the
party, so eat up, drink up, and
smoke up. They turn the music up and
start partying. The first to arrive
at the party is an off duty
detective Jamal Steals.

Jamal Steals met War in prison.
He was the correctional officer on
War's tier. They became cool over
time. Officer Steals was fresh out
of the police academy when War was
in prison.

He was smuggling in weed for War at first, but when War met Juker, he started bringing in cocaine. That is also were Juker met Jason. Jason was released three years earlier than Juker, so he never meet War.

Jamal Steals finished the academy the same year his older brother Tony Steals was accepted into the F.B.I. Right now they all are waiting on Juker and Al to start the meeting. War is looking for, and asking around for Rickie, but no one has seen him.

So War calls his cellphone, and Rickie answers, "Yo what up?" War says, "I was just looking for you. You did not forget about the party did you?" Rickie says, "No, I will be there later on. But right now I just heard your name come out somebody's mouth and from the looks of it, they gave the nigga a gun. War asks Rickie, "Where are you?" Rickie says, "I am at the club. I am going to see what is going on. Let me call you back."

Rickie walks up to Doevee and asks, "Who was the guy you were speaking with?" "That was Joe. He came to pick up a burner for his brother."

So Rickie inquires about the
brother as well. Doevee says, "Damn
nigga, you the police?" Rickie says,
"No man, I thought I heard and saw
y'all say War's name, and you give
him a gun. War is my boy, so I am
trying to see what is going on."

Doevee says, "Well if you must
know. Joe's brother's name is ToTo.
That is my homie, he good. He let me
use a gun a while back. So I was
paying him back."

Doevee says, "But you did hear
War's name. Joe told me To-To is
giving the gun to Tyson. He asked if
I thought War had something to do
with Tyson's house being shot up. I
told him no."

Rickie asks, "Does Tyson think
War shot up his house? Because that
dude is unpredictable." "I don't
know about that," Doevee says.

Rickie calls War back on his
cellphone and tells him that Tyson
may be looking for him. War pauses
and says, "I don`t know a Tyson. Did
I do something to him or hurt
someone he knows or something like
that?"

Rickie says, "His house got shot
up the other day, and he is looking

for answers I guess." War says to Rickie, "Well, if he thinks I did it, take him out." They hang up the phone, and Rickie leaves the club without saying a word.

Trina is at the house alone. She took Corey over to a friends house, so she can mentally prepare for the big talk with Lou.

Meanwhile, Lou is still at his Uncle Bowe's house. Ronnie and Lou are on the phone, and Trell is playing chess with Bowe. Lou gets off the phone and tells the crew the news.

He tells everyone that Al is not using him to sell his product. Trell asks, "For clarity, is that a good thing, or a bad thing?" Lou says, "A good thing for me, but bad for my Lil homies. I already told them that I had a big shipment coming in."

Trell says, "Now, tell them Lil niggas that it is not coming in. It's over." Bowe says to Lou, "As of now, you are out the game. You do not have a connection to the product anymore. You won nephew. Lou says, "I guess I did. I did not see it like that."

Ronnie hangs up the phone with his wife, looks, at Lou and asks, "What did you do? Talk nigga?" Lou says, "Man I did not do anything. He said I was too hot to deal with, my face all on the news, and everything that comes with it.

Bowe says, "Al is a smart businessman. I could find nothing on him. Lou says, "So he was lying about being hot. His Nephew has a crew down here. He is taking over for him now."

Before I got off the phone with Al, "He asked me the name of the player I wanted him to hit. I told him a guy name War. Would you believe he ask me to stand down."

Trell says, "What do you mean stand down, this the military are something?" Lou says, "Once I told him the guys name, he came clean. War is the dude his nephew is working with."

Trell looks at Lou and says, "Then what is next?"

Al is setting up a sit down with him tomorrow. Ronnie says, "So just like that it is over?" Lou says, "Not yet, I need to see how that meeting goes with Juker."

A smile beams across Ronnie's face now that he knows the whole story. "Well guys, it has been real, and it has been fun. It just hasn't been real fun. I am going home. I think we are all good to go now. I called a yellow cab it will be here in ten minutes."

Lou says, "I could have given you a ride home. Ronnie replies, "I am going to the boxing gym to get my car first. I`m good! And the next time you need a ride, I think you should do the same, and call yourself a cab, Uber, Lyft, or something."

Ten minutes later, Ronnie is on the way home to see his family. When he arrives Detective Cobb pulls up right behind his car and blocks him in the driveway.

Detective Cobb says that he just wanted to let Ronnie know that he is wanted for questioning. Ronnie says, "Damn man, at least let me go talk to my wife first."

Cobb says, "Alright, but make it quick." Ronnie asks, "Do I have to go down there for questioning? Can't we talk here?" "You know I can not do that, it has to be on the record."

Lou is sitting outside of his house in the car with Trell, and dreading the meeting with Trina. Trell says, "I support any decision you make. You can not go wrong with this one. I am going to go to the bar and have a few drinks."

They both get out of the car. Trell gets into the driver's seat and Lou goes inside.

Trina is in the bathroom when Lou enters the house. Lou goes into the kitchen and makes himself a drink. Trina walks out of the bathroom, and sees Lou in the kitchen. Trina says, "I did not hear you come in." Lou says, "Oh."

Trina says, "Are you going to leave me? I guess you already know?" "I do not know what I wanna do right now," he says. "I am sorry for what I put you through. I was a little girl when we meet. Yeah, I was by myself when we meet, but my boyfriend was in the other car with his brother, War. War knew you had money. He convinced my boyfriend to have me set you up. I knew I could lose you one way or the other, but if I did not tell you what was going

on your life would be on the line.
Does that mean anything?"

Lou says, "I am glad you told me
the truth, but you tried to have me
killed."

Trina says, "I did not know you
at that time. Since I have been with
you I have been so happy." "I do not
know if I am ready to trust you
right now Trina." "This is a man's
world, I was only surviving in it.
You showed me so much, and Corey is
crazy over you," she says.

Lou says, "I need some time to
think." Trina says, "Do what your
heart says to do." "I do not use my
heart to make important decisions. I
use my head. And if you were a dude,
I would have killed you by now. I
have been making love to you almost
every day since we meet. What else
have you lied to me about?"

Trina says, "So are we staying
together or what? "What the fuck do
you mean, or what?" Trina says,
"What are you trying to do? You want
me to pack my things or what?"

Trina is using Tina's advice to
be herself, but Lou is taking it
like she does not care about what
happens. He kind of feels like she

won, she got away with something she
could die for.
Trell is pulling up in the
driveway. He texts Lou that he is
outside. Trina is still talking like
she does not care about what Lou
does. She will be straight either
way the coin lands. Lou walks out of
the house without saying a word and
gets into his car.

Trell is now back in the
passenger seat. Lou grabs his gun
from under the driver's seat goes
back into the house, and puts four
bullets into Trina`s chest, when he
hears, "Lou you alright?"

Lou snaps out of his trance.
Trell says, "You alright dude?"
"Yeah, I`m good." He grabs his gun
from under the seat. Trell says to
Lou, "Are you sure about this?"

Lou does not say anything. He
just gets out of the car and walks
back into the house.

Trell is nervously in the car
like, man, I should stop this. He is
just waiting on the sound of the
gunshots.

Lou rushes back into the house
to find Trina broken down crying.

She has her head down on the table
her face is inside her arms.

She does not see Lou looking
down at her with a 45 magnum in his
hands. Lou sees that she is not only
regretting what she did, but she is
devastated. He walks out of the
house.

Lou gets back into the car and
drives off. Trell says, "Well did
you." Lou says, "No." Trell was
relieved. "It is hard to hurt people
you love."

Lou says, "She was my only
reason to quit the game. Now that I
am out. All my goals, dreams, and
fantasy's... she is apart of them...
being on my side. Know matter what I
do, it will never be a dream come
true without her."

Trell says, "I am glad you
didn't kill her. I would have felt
like I encouraged it. "Lou says, "I
am glad that you came back when you
did." Trell says, "I had to... some
dude got killed at the bar." Lou
asks, "Just now?" "Yes. I was
seating down drinking a beer. I
heard like nine shots. I waited five
minutes, then I left the bar as the
police arrived."

Trina calls Lora immediately after she sees Lou drive off. She tells Lora she thought he was about to kill her. She watched him from the front window as he went to the car and grab his gun.

"As he started walking back towards the house, I ran back into the kitchen, put my head down, and started to cry as hard as I could. Lou is weak for tears."

Lora says, "Girl you are living to dangerous." Trina says, "Well it worked, and I am still alive... but now I think I might be pregnant. I have been throwing up for the last few days."

Lora says, "So if you are, are you going to keep it?" Trina says, "Yes. Even if he does not want me to. This baby may be the glue for us to get over this situation. Lou will make a great dad, but I just have to show him I have his back. This baby will help. Trina says, I want to smoke a blunt before I find out if I am pregnant though. You have some weed. Lora says, "Yes, I do. You coming over." Trina says, "Yes, I am on my way."

Conclusion

Later on that night, Ryder is outside with Tank and Money, when he receives a call from Toya. She says that she was on the phone with Tyson, when she heard a bunch of gunshots. I think someone just killed my brother. Ryder asks about Tyson's whereabouts, but she did not know.

Ryder says, "Ok I will find out what is going on. When I do, I will call you." Ryder takes a moment to think, before hanging up, and then says, "You know what? I am going to come pick you up tonight ok." Toya agrees, and they hang up the phone. Ryder tells Tank and Money what Toya just told him.

Tank says, "Let's go see what is going on around the hood." Ryder replies, "Now why would you want to go and do that? We wanted him dead also." Ryder sees this moment as a revelation. "Someone just solved our only problem," He continues.

"Right, so why be seen out there looking around? We good right here," Money adds. "You are thinking like a grown man," Tank says. "But I, am a grown fool. Ryder says, "That shit, makes no sense." The three of them joke around enjoying the night.

Rickie is now at the Juker's party. He has been waiting for his chance to speak with War alone.

War is chatting with Juker and Jamal at the moment, he is telling them a story about how he got the nickname War. War tells them that his grandmother gave him that nickname after the Village People...

..."You know, the song. War what is it good for, huh! My grandmother loved to watch me sing that song as a kid, and the name just stuck after that...

...nowadays people think it is because I like to war out there in the streets. I do not even know who that guy is," War says. "Well, ever since you been out, homebodies have been dropping," Jamal says.

War says, "Since I got back home, all I did was shoot up one car. But I thought it was Lou. How was I supposed to know that two high school kids stole his car? I messed up, I know. But he had my brother killed. How lucky can one guy be? I took a shot at him ten years ago, and I lost my brother."

Rickie asks, "I thought the police killed your brother?" "The police did kill my brother," War said. "We were at Lou`s house. My brother's girl, Trina, set it all up."

"Wait, Trina is Lou`s girl? Rickie asks." This is an obvious sticking point with War, so he gathers his internal anger to say, "No. Trina set up the robbery." Rickie says, "That is my girl's best friend. Well, she just broke up with me, but Trina is still with the dude." "She never left that dude after all of these years?" War asks. Rickie replies, "Nope." War says, "I want to talk to her. Whenever she comes over by your girl's house call me."

"So let me ask you something, Juker's Texas accent seemed to become more pronounced when he looks into War's eyes, and says, "You telling me Lou never did anything to you, and you are trying to kill him?" "He killed my brother," War says." Juker says, "No War, he did not kill your brother. It is all in your head, because deep down, you know that part of what happened to your brother is on you. Who planned the robbery?"

War would not normally let anyone
speak to him this way, but he
recognizes that Juker is speaking
the truth. "I did," he says.

"Your brother died by the hands of
the police. Now, does Lou know that
it is you shooting at him?" Juker
asks. War says, "I don't know. Does
Trina know?"

Then he turns to Rickie, "Did you
tell your girl anything?" Rickie
says, "Huh." "You did, didn't you,"
War says. Rickie's subdued demeanor
signals to War that he did tell Lora
about War. "Now he may be looking
for me," War says.

Juker says, "He is not, at least,
not anymore. My uncle told him not
to make any moves on you. Because we
are working together. I am meeting
with him tomorrow."

War says, "I can take my shot then."
"My uncle made a deal with him to
keep the peace so let's not make my
uncle mad, please. He likes Lou. Lou
has always come through for him in
the past... besides, making money is
way better than making war, is what
my uncle believes in.

He looks at War with a serious
demeanor and says, "It is over with

you and Lou." War says, "Just like that. So I should just relax because your uncle told him not to make a move on me. I robbed him, and shot up his car." "Yeah, but you missed both times," Juker says.

Jamal says, "He is right, let it go. We have a big shipment coming in tomorrow. Let's focus on making our money ok." Jamal says, "You'll are making my job much harder with all of these killings. I am only one cop. I can only do so much." They all share a look of agreement with these business terms.

Lou and Trell are back at Bowe`s. Trell says to Lou as they pull up, "Is that Ronnie`s car parked in the driveway." Lou replies, "I think so."

The two of them walk inside of the house. They were right, Ronnie is in the house talking to uncle Bowe. Ronnie looks at the two of them and says, "What`s up killers?"

Trell says, "There you go again." Ronnie says, "No. There you'll go again. Just be lucky I am built for this." Lou turns to Bowe and says, "What is this fool talking about?" Bowe looks at Ronnie, and says, "Go

ahead and tell them what happened
today."

Ronnie says, "I was picked up by
Cobb; again." "So why are you free?
What did they want?" Trell asks.
"Well, I am free because I didn't do
shit. And they were not looking for
me." He turns to Trell to say. "They
wanted you at first. But my story
checked out, and now we are all off
the hook."

Trell asks, "What did you tell
them?" Ronnie says, "The truth. My
daughter had already told them that
you were driving her car. They
showed me a video of Trell using the
payphone. They asked me who was the
driver. I told them me. They asked
who was on the payphone. I said we
were calling a number that was on
our dead friend's cellphone. Then he
asked where did we go after that, I
told him to my house. To get my car,
and that I had some running around
to do. Trell took my daughter's car
to pick up Lou to go get a rental
car."

Ronnie is very proud of his
performance at the police station,
and it is obvious in his voice when
he says...

"That is when I flipped the script on his ass. I said, you must have forgotten that Lou's car was shot up, with two dead kids inside. We are the victims here... those assholes. Do you know that we even went all the way out to the rental car place to see if I was lying before he released me? So Trell, your name is clear because of me. Lou, you are in the clear also. I saved the day once again...

...but before I left, he told me that the number that you called was to the cellphone of a dead police officer. And that is also a link to your car being stolen, Lou. Plus he said your friend Jason was in direct contact with the two officers before they were murdered, and that if I needed any help to call him, because they are there to protect and serve. I said, can I please go now. I did not want to hear that bull crap."

Trell says to Ronnie, "Let me find out you wearing a wire. Nigga, you said too much to those people already." "To hell with you, "Ronnie yells back. Lou says, "Y`all calm down, it seems to me that it worked itself out. So we are good." Ronnie says, "It has been a long five days, and I am glad all of this shit is

over with. I am going home to my
family."

Trell says, "That is the best thing
you said all day. I am going home
too." Ronnie asks Lou, "What are you
going to do?" "As of now, I do not
know. But for now, I will spend the
night here. I am going to meet with
Al`s nephew tomorrow. I'll catch up
with you guys. Thanks for all the
help."

Trell and Ronnie leave the house.
Bowe and Lou talk for a few more
hours before they prepare for bed.
Bowe gets up to make his exit before
he says to Lou, "If you think she
loves you. Let it go! Otherwise, you
will have to break your own heart to
hurt Trina. Go back home!" Bowe
starts to walk up the stairs. "Good
night Nephew," he adds. Lou replies
with, "Good night Unc'."
The next day Lou meets with Juker at
the same restaurant he used to meet
Al in all those times. It is a hot
summer Thursday afternoon. Lou does
not know much about Juker other than
he is Big Al's nephew.

Juker asks Lou, "What is this
meeting about? My uncle did not say
anything to me about giving you
anything."

Lou says, "Well, your uncle told me that he would be giving the shipment that is coming in, to me. But by my face being on the news, and detectives hanging around. I was too hot to deal with."

Lou adds, "So he gave you a chance to make your own money. I am cool with all of that."

Juker does not understand what Lou is trying to say, so Lou tries a different approach to reach Juker without being disrespectful.

"I promised my crew the work already and they are waiting on it. They count on me to eat to feed their family. I am out of the game, to be honest, I just needed to work out a deal with you," Lou says.

Juker asks, "And why should I make a deal with you?" Lou replies, "Because War shot up my car and killed those two kids. Your uncle asked me not to move on him. It is that dude's fault that you are working with him, and why I am not getting that shipment."

Juker says, "Can I tell you something? No, let me show you something." Juker hands Lou an envelope with pictures of him and

Trell. Juker says, "I know you'll have something to do with getting them killed. I told them to follow you. But my uncle does not know about that. I guess it is karma. They killed J rock..."

Juker seems to have real compassion for J Rock. "I never got a chance to ask what happened thanks to you. That was my boy. I do not understand that one," Juker says. "Wait, are you talking about Jason?" Lou asks. "Was he killed in his house?" Lou continues. "Yes," Juker replies.

Lou says, "So we were right, that number did kill Jason." Juker asks, "You know Jason? Lou says, "That is my homie." "We were going there to talk numbers for this shipment to see how much we needed," Juker says. "He was excited about the phone call that morning," Lou adds.

Lou feels validated by Juker's words.

Juker says, "Well, you already have your revenge on who killed your homie. I feel bad also, I should have gone there myself. So on the strength of Jason, I can give you five bricks a month for only twenty thousand. If you need more than that thirty thousand per."

Lou says, "That is fair, I like it. Deal!" Juker says, "I have to go I will call you once I am ready for the money. So just have it ready. Just be ready." Lou says, "I am not going to be there all of the time. This is my last time meeting with you about this product. I will introduce you to my crew. They are good to work with."

Juker says, "They are not going to meet me either. War has a runner. So whoever he asks to deal with them, that person will be the main one to deal with them."

Juker looks at Lou and says, "Any deal we make today is over if your people try some funny shit." Lou says, "You are starting to sound like Al. No funny shit, I got you."

Lou calls Ryder immediately after he meets with Juker. He tells him that they need to meet up. Ryder asks if he can come to his spot. Lou replies, "I am on my way." Lou was at Ryder house within ten minutes.

Tank, Money, and Ryder are outside. Lou gets out of the car. He tells the crew about the deal he just made. He needs one hundred thousand dollars.

Ryder says to Lou, "I do not do it anymore." Money says, "I have a baby on the way, and we want to start up a night club. Lou says, Well cool, we all good then. Tank says, "I will do it." Ryder looks at him and says, "You do not have the clientele to move one brick."

Tank says, "I don`t but Lil Duegie and Byron do. I can only serve them and still eat like crazy.

Lou says, "How much are you going to charge them per brick thirty thousand dollars. So I will make fifty thousand a flip. Lou asks, "What if they need more the five a month?" Tank says, "I will go up to five thousand dollars until next month." Lou says to Tank, "Never change your number. Just be happy with the fifty thousand dollars a month. Just let them get it for what you getting it for until next month."

Tank says, "That is dumb. I am not working for free. If my number has to stay the same. I will charge them thirty-one thousand then. Lou says, "You know what, that is a good ideal. Now you are ready for business. You have the one hundred thousand." Tanks says "I have fifty thousand. Lou says to Ryder, "How do you feel about him moving weight?" Ryder says, "He will be good I will be watching over him. As long as he deals with Lil Duegie and Byron, he will be alright. I will put the other fifty thousand on it.

Lou says to the crew. This is an introduction. You do not need to pay me anything. You will deal with the person you will meet. So stay by the phone we move on a phone call. I will meet you'll where ever they ask us to meet.

Lou leaves Ryder`s house and goes home. Trina is not there. So he leaves the house and drives over to Sabrina`s house. He parks a few houses up the street from Sabrina's house, and watches from a distance.

Lou gets a call from Trell. Trell ask Lou what he is up to, and then Lou tells him that he is stalking Trina. He whispers, "I am outside Sabrina`s house. Trell starts to hysterically laughing. "Well, when you are done, give me a call. I have some fireweed that I just got. Come smoke with me."

But before they hang up the phone, Trell tells Lou, "Don`t do anything stupid." Lou says, "I`m not just

seeing what she is up to". Trell
says, see what she is up to? Man,
just call the girl. I`ll be at the
house." Trell hangs up he phone. Lou
sits outside of Sabrina's house in
the car for almost two hours before
he leaves to go to Trell's house.

Lou arrives around 5 pm. Trell says,
"It took you long enough." Lou says,
"I had to take care of some
business." "If stalking your girl is
business. How did that work out for
you? Trell asks. Lou says, "Ok, I
guess". Trell replies, "I was
joking. What did you do Lou?" Lou
smiles. Lou asks Trell to roll a
blunt because he is ready to smoke.
The two friends smoke all night. Lou
told him all he did after they hung
up the phone.

The next day Lou gets up and head
back to the house. When he arrives
he sees Corey outside talking to
Zap. Corey says high to Lou as if
things are normal, and Lou walks
inside to find Trina watching
television.

Trina asks, "Can Lora come over.?"
Lou replies, "Since when couldn't
she come over." Trina says, "I did
not mean it like that. Her boyfriend
was killed yesterday. She does not
want to be at that house right now."

Lou asks Trina, "Who was her boyfriend," and Trina says, "His name was Rickie."

Tank and Ryder are alone on the front porch. Tank tells Ryder that Bam told him that he saw Lou around Sabrina's house yesterday. Bam said he was just parked down the street from the house. Ryder asks, "Why are you telling me this?" Tank replies, "Because Lora's boyfriend was killed around there yesterday. Ryder says, "Tank, tell Bam don`t be speaking on that to nobody." Tank replies, You think people are stupid huh?

Ryder ignores him, and says, "Byron called, he is on his way to pick up two bricks." That brings a Colgate smile to Tank's face. Lou gave all of this up?" Tank thinks to himself. He starts to mouth the words that are "sixty-two thousand dollars".

Tank thinks of all of the mouths that he can feed out of that money.

War, Juker, and Jamal Steals are having a conversation about Rickie's murder. War says, "I think Lou did it." "There you go again with that Lou shit. Lou is clean in all this, we, have a deal.

"Besides, I met with him twice yesterday. He is out of the game now," Juker concludes. "Then who do you think did it?" War asks. Juker says, I do not know.

Jamal says, "The streets will start talking sooner or later. But we need to stop the killing for now. Way too much in one week." War says, "I did not kill anyone." Jamal says, "So you are not counting those kids?" War says, "I am counting them... how many times am I going to have to say that I messed that one up...

...but I am saying, no one else got hurt. I have been chillin' on the killin'."

Juker turns to Jamal, and asks, "Did you take care of the evidence." Jamal replies, "It was not easy, but I got it done."

War says to Jamal, "Looks like we all did some damage." Jamal replies, "Well, the streets are giving you all of the credit." "Yeah, but only because of my nickname," War adds.

Trina and Lou are upstairs in the bedroom talking. Trina asks Lou if they still together since he has not spoken a word about it. Lou is trying not to think about his situation, as if it will magically go away. But deep down he knows he has to confront his feelings.

Trina says, "Well, are we." Lou says, "What do you think?" "I don`t know. I mean you haven't even touched me." Lou says, "I think I want you, but I feel like I do not know you. I do not know how to kick you out yet." Trina says, "Ask me anything, I will not lie." Lou says, "Ok. Let's just take it one day at a time. Trina says to Lou, "Lou. I am pregnant." Lou turns his head to look Trina in her eyes.

Meanwhile, Detective Cobb is trying to make sense of all of these cases. He has Lou and his crew's photo pinned on the wall. Jason's deceased photo, tied to the two dead officers, which, are tied back to Lou, and the two dead teens.

So Detective Cobb needs to take another look at the evidence from Jason`s death. He takes a walk to the evidence room. Cobb gives the clerk the information for the case file, and after walking away for a moment, the clerk hands Cobb a box containing all of the evidence.

Cobb sees that the box has been tampered with. When he looks inside

he notices that someone has
destroyed the evidence.

Cobb is pissed off now. Ever since
Lou got away the first time, he has
been waiting for his chance for
another shot at convicting him.

He asks to look at the case file
from ten years ago, the night that
Lou's house was raided. He looks at
the names of all the cops involved
in the raid first. Some of them are
no longer on the force.

Cobb sees that the only officer that
fired their gun outside of the house
the night that War's younger brother
was killed is Tony Steals.

Cobb hopes that Detective Walker did
not speak about the case to her
partner, because even a harmless
conversation between partners can be
enough for a corrupt officer to do
damage. If so, they already know
that he is looking into the two
shootings.

Cobb will start his investigation
into the Steals brothers. He first
needs to find someone in the F.B.I
that he can trust.

You see, the streets have no ending.
It is a cycle that goes on and on,

and neither this book nor any other could ever explain it fully.

Perception is reality. Do you think Lou killed Lora's boyfriend Rickie? Do you think Rickie killed Tyson? Sometimes people throw bricks and hide their hands, and end up hitting the wrong person.

Murder, in some cases, is something that must be done when living in the ghetto. Decisions are being made all of the time to murder another person based on assumptions. Especially once a person starts to see their own friend's dying. This cycle normally begins around the teenage years.

If you see your friends going to jail, or getting murdered one by one. It changes you. Once a teen tastes and feels the power of making a lot of money. He or she now sees school as a waste of time. Now, every time they go to school they are missing out on making money. How can some politician fix that? They can't. And yet, words are uttered that promise futures that never seem to come.

Rich or poor, black, brown, or lighter tone, we all share the same emotions although we may express

them differently, we all have the
same color blood, but we may bleed
it differently, and yet, with all of
our commonality, some among us,
choose to focus on what is different
about ourselves, instead of building
upon what is right with us.

Classism is a nasty little virus
that mingles among us that keeps the
haves as the have nots, and keeps
the have some's trying to keep up
with the Jones'. This is not an
insult to capitalism as much as it
is a pointing towards its ugly
offspring... greed, self indulgence,
and a lack of moral fiber.

Money is so powerful that it can
make a weak person kill a sibling or
parent, take solace in the pain of
others, steal and fight over
inheritance money, or what little is
left behind. It can be good or evil,
depending on who is telling the
story.

The first person to put money in a
child's hands has the power over
that soul. The parent always has the
first chance.

The End

Kentrell Myers

is a music producer and author, born and raised in New Orleans and owner of Blackkkash Music since 2013.

Mr. Myers was raised in a musical family, and traveled on the road with his father from 13-16 years old and credits this period as crucial in his life.

He finished high school at George Washington Carver in New Orleans, fathered two daughters, and became a member of the IBEW electrician's union.

Mr. Myers has lived in Jacksonville, Florida, Akron and Columbus, Ohio, and Indianapolis, Indiana.

Five years into his Electrician Apprenticing he decided to take music more seriously, and eventually started Blackkkash Music..

Michael Gerald

is a professional writer, producer, and director
with over twenty years of entertainment industry experience.

Born in New Orleans, Louisiana, he attended the prestigious
St. Augustine High School, before traveling the world in the
United States Navy. Japan, Thailand, Singapore, UAE, Philippines,
Morocco, and Mexico are just a few of the places he has visited
during his travels.

In 2008, Mr. Gerald, got his first feature movie directorial opportunity
with a suspense drama he co-wrote, entitled, "Unchained Melody".
Since then he has directed and produced music videos, documentaries,
and other non-scripted content.

He is also co-owner of 5Picture Films, and independent film
production company.

www.ingramcontent.com/pod-product-compliance
Lightning Source LLC
Chambersburg PA
CBHW030300200626
46816CB00002BA/714